Read all the books about Madison Finn!

From the Files of Madison Finn

Lost and Found

By Laura Dower

HYPERION
New York

Text copyright © 2002 by Laura Dower

From the Files of Madison Finn, Volo, and the Volo colophon are trademarks of Disney Enterprises, Inc.

Printed in the United States of America

First Edition
5 7 9 10 8 6 4

The main body of text of this book is set in 13-point Frutiger Roman.

ISBN 0-7868-1558-2

Visit www.madisonfinn.com

For Emma Silverman-Keates, Emily Remmers, and Maija Fiedelholtz—three future Madisons who sparkle with life and joy

Chapter 1

No matter how hard she shoved, Madison couldn't squeeze all her stuff into the teeny green gym locker. She had hated gym class from the moment seventh grade started. Before the winter holidays, Madison's gym class was scheduled in the afternoon. Now, gym was in the morning, first period on Mondays.

The worst part was wearing the dreaded gym uniform. Its ugly blue polyester gym shorts made Madison's legs itch, and a too tight, white T-shirt with a blue Far Hills Junior High logo was not exactly the most flattering fashion statement. And wearing that shirt meant wearing a bra, even though Madison didn't have much to fill it out.

And even *worse* than wearing a scary,

1

see-through T-shirt was the fact that Hart Jones would see her looking that way. Hart, Madison's big crush at school, just happened to be in her same gym section. He would see her wearing the ugly outfit.

Madison had to stop herself from over-thinking immediately. She sighed and took a seat on the small benches between locker banks. *Hart Jones.* Just the idea of him made her feel faint. Or was that because the locker room smelled like wet rubber floor mats and soccer balls?

She pulled her sweater over her head and wriggled into her T-shirt. Then she carefully yanked off her stockings and tugged on the polyester shorts under her wool skirt. They felt snugger than snug, and her legs prickled with goose bumps from the chilly air.

The locker area wasn't very full, so no one had seen her change. That was a major relief. Madison was standing alone in her row. Madison's homeroom had been dismissed early. Sometimes homeroom teachers let certain groups out earlier than others. However, neither of her best friends, Aimee or Fiona, had arrived from her homeroom yet.

Madison heard whispering in the next locker bank but didn't think much of it at first. Then she heard someone say *her* name.

"I can't believe I still have Madison Finn as my partner," the person grumbled with a huff.

Madison knew the voice. It was Poison Ivy Daly, her mortal enemy.

Ivy was speaking about their science lab. Mr. Danehy had assigned Madison and Ivy as lab partners. He obviously didn't know how much they didn't get along.

"Just ignore her," Ivy's friend Rose advised. "What's the big deal?"

Madison stood on top of the bench, leaning into the lockers, to hear whatever more she could hear. Ivy was talking to her drones, Rose Thorn and Phony Joanie. Madison knew they might say not-so-nice stuff, but she still wanted to hear it. Unfortunately, the juicy eavesdropping stopped there. Madison's name wasn't mentioned again. They moved on to talking about hair. Ivy always wore her perfect red hair in perfect red clips.

As Madison stepped off the bench, the room got very quiet. Madison was surprised to see someone standing in the space between the locker banks. It was Ivy. And she was staring right at Madison.

"Hello, Madison," Ivy said curtly. "I didn't know you were in here."

"Yeah, well . . ." Madison mumbled. She turned back to the green locker.

Madison wondered if, even for a fleeting second, Ivy felt a smidge guilty about gossiping without knowing who was nearby. But clearly Ivy felt nothing of the sort. She just *stared*. Madison felt Ivy's eyes watching her.

Rose and Joanie appeared from around the corner, too.

"Nice shorts," Joanie snapped to Madison. She was always snappy.

Madison felt her entire body shrink when Joanie said the words, however. *Nice shorts.* Ivy, Rose, and Joanie were wearing their shorts baggy and longer. They made the uniform look good. But Madison stood there in gym shorts one size too small.

"'Scuse me!" Aimee Gillespie said, appearing from nowhere and sliding past the others into Madison's locker bank. Best friends have a way of showing up just at the right time. "Hey, Maddie!" she chirped.

Ivy raised one eyebrow at Aimee's entrance and walked away to find a mirror. Her drones followed.

"What was that about?" Aimee asked Madison.

Madison sat down on the bench again. Her shorts felt tighter than ever now. "These." She pointed to them.

"Huh?" Aimee shrugged. "Not everyone got the new shorts, I don't think. It doesn't really matter, does—"

"*New* shorts?" Madison asked incredulously. "*What* new shorts?"

Aimee explained that a letter had been mailed home with an order form for a new style of gym shorts. The administration had received complaints about the sizes being too small for a lot of girls. They were offering a new style.

"I never knew," Madison said. Her mom must

have thrown out the mail without reading it. She did that sometimes.

"But you look great in those shorts," Aimee said. "You have nice legs."

"Thanks," Madison said. Maybe the shorts weren't so bad after all.

Fiona appeared with a flounce and a smile. "Helloooooo! Did you guys have a good weekend?"

She'd already changed into her gym uniform, pulling off her clothes to reveal the shorts underneath her pants. Fiona said it was easier to change that way. Of course she had on the loose shorts.

"Where did you get those?" Madison asked her.

"I don't know," Fiona admitted, a little spaced out. She sneezed. "They're more comfy than the other ones."

Madison would have to ask Mom to order her a pair of those.

"GIRLS!" A booming voice echoed into the locker room. Coach Hammond blew her whistle for emphasis. "LET'S GO! LET'S GO! INTO THE GYM!"

She wasn't as mean as a drill sergeant, but Coach Hammond was strict about starting class on time, lining up in perfect rows, and playing fair.

Madison hid behind Aimee and Fiona as they shuffled into the main part of the gym. She was happier than happy to see a few other girls wearing the shorter, snugger shorts.

"OKAY!" Coach Hammond yelled. She yelled

even when she was standing nose to nose with a student. "TODAY WE HAVE PHYSICAL FITNESS TESTING! HEADS UP!"

Aimee turned to Madison. "This stinks. It's Monday morning. Who tests your physical fitness on Monday?"

"Yeah." Fiona sniffled. Then she sneezed three times in a row.

Madison sat down on the floor between her friends, pretending to listen and watch Coach Hammond. But her eyes were wandering over to Hart. He was looking hunky, lying on his side across from them, whispering to Chet Waters, his new best friend and Fiona's twin brother.

"UPSY DAISY, BOYS AND GIRLS," Coach Hammond commanded. "EVERYONE UP AND INTO NEAT ROWS, PLEASE. WE NEED TO TEST YOUR AGILITY AND SPEED."

Coach didn't call it a race against each other, but kids pretended like it was. Everyone in the first row was paired up with someone in the second row.

Boys mostly paired with boys, except for Fiona and Chet, who led off the rows. They wanted to race each other for the obvious reason.

Coach Hammond didn't hear their friendly exchange.

"Eat my dust," Chet whispered to his sister.

Fiona smirked. "You—ah-ah . . . *choo*!" she said, sneezing again. "You *wish*."

6

Coach Hammond explained that the task was to run up and down the length of the gym three times, then weave through the orange cones at the side of the room and run three more times up and back in the gym.

"I'm tired just thinking about that," moaned Hart. He was standing right behind Madison.

"ON YOUR MARK, GET SET . . . GO!" Coach Hammond blew the whistle, and Fiona and Chet took off for the other side of the gym.

Madison couldn't exactly remember what she had to do during past fitness tests in middle school, but they had certainly never been like this. Kids were cheering on other kids, like it was a sporting event.

"Go! Go! GO!"

As Fiona made the turn to come back toward the group the second time, she tripped and fell to the floor.

"Ahhhhh!" a bunch of girls, including Madison, screamed.

Coach Hammond shooed them away and helped Fiona to her feet.

Fiona rubbed her elbows, which had slammed into the floor. She started to cough. "I feel hot, Coach."

She was *burning* hot, as it turned out. So the feverish Fiona was sent to the nurse. She waved to Madison and Aimee as she left the gym.

I hope she's really okay, Madison thought.

"LET'S GET BACK IN LINE, BOYS AND GIRLS,"

Coach Hammond ordered. Everyone obeyed. The paired-off test subjects started up again.

Years of ballerina twirls helped Aimee to pass the fitness test easily. She was fast *and* graceful. Her running companion was some girl Madison only knew a little. The girl had to stop halfway through the test to take a big puff from her inhaler. She was one of two asthmatics in the class, but she still passed the test.

Most kids passed. When their turns came, boys and girls sped up and down the gym without even breaking a sweat.

Madison always knew she was good at running, or at least she was good at running *away*. But right there in the heat of the moment, she was losing her nerve. She had a fear that she would be the one to *not* pass. She'd be the one who fell into a sweaty, lumpy pile.

She looked over to see who'd be racing by her side. It was Ivy, who made a face.

Madison leaned over to retie her sneaker. Out of the corner of her eye, she caught Hart looking her way, too. She thought he was smiling a little.

"Hey, Finnster," he called out.

Some kids giggled at the nickname.

Madison gulped.

"ON YOUR MARK, GET SET . . ."

As soon as Coach Hammond screeched "GO," Madison was off and zipping across the gym. She didn't pay attention to how fast Ivy was going.

She turned at the first wall and never looked back. Even when an orange cone got knocked over in the middle of the test, Madison ran on. She huffed and puffed as she finished up. . . .

"IT'S A TIE!" Coach Hammond wailed.

Madison looked over at Ivy as they walked over to the sidelines, expecting her to grimace or pout or make her poisonous sneer.

But Ivy *smiled* instead.

"That was wicked hard," Ivy said, breathing heavily. She walked away.

Madison shook her head and adjusted her shorts to make them a little bit longer. Seventh grade could be wicked hard.

"I hope Fiona's not really, really sick," Aimee whispered to Madison as they changed back into their school clothes in the locker room after gym ended. "Oh my God, what if she is really, really sick?"

"She isn't," Madison said, hoping that her friend was okay. She pulled on her stockings leg by leg. "Nurse Shim probably already called her mom."

"Let's call her later," Aimee suggested.

Madison grabbed her things out of the teeny green gym locker and climbed the stairs up toward the computer center. Her math textbook felt heavier than heavy inside her bag. Madison had a giant exam coming up the next day; she had barely reviewed the first half of the chapter.

When Madison walked into Mrs. Wing's classroom, she found her favorite teacher sitting at her desk. She was looking out the window at the dark, blue-gray sky.

"Looks like stormy weather," Mrs. Wing said softly, her glass-bead earrings jingling as she turned her head to face Madison. "Looks like snow."

Madison sat down at her desk. "Cool!"

Mrs. Wing chuckled. "I don't like this cold. Winter is my least-favorite season. Brrrr." She faked a dramatic shiver.

"Mrs. Wing, do I need to come after school today to help with the Web site?" Madison asked, changing the subject. She had signed on to help as an assistant school cybrarian, which meant inputting polls, answering questions, helping to keep the school data, and more. Lately extra-credit homework and volunteering at the Far Hills Animal Shelter took preference over the Web, but Madison wanted to start working on the computer more.

"I was speaking with Walter about helping with the data entry," Mrs. Wing said. "And Drew, too. There's always room for helpers."

Walter Diaz, otherwise known as Egg, was Madison's best guy friend. And Drew Maxwell was Egg's best friend and therefore Madison's friend, too, by association. Not only were the two boys into computers as much as (if not more than) Madison, but they had their own Web page development in

10

progress. Madison wanted to build her own site one day, too.

"So what are we adding to the site?" Madison asked Mrs. Wing.

Mrs. Wing smiled. "I want to add a Winter Wonderland section with news about hockey games and winter festivals and everything else going on inside and outside the school."

"What's up, Maddie?" Egg called out as he strolled into the computer lab. "What are you doing here so early?"

The second-period bell rang, and Drew walked into class along with everyone else. "Hey, Maddie," he said, sliding into a desk and giving her a wave.

While Mrs. Wing got the rest of the class settled, Egg talked nonstop about his new skates.

"I just got these killer hockey skates," he boasted. One of Egg's greatest goals in life was to play for the New York Rangers hockey team. "I can't wait to try them out. They're black with silver stripes on the side."

"Like racing stripes," Drew quipped. "You wearing them tomorrow?"

"What's tomorrow?" Madison asked.

Egg gasped like he'd just been punched. "Oh, man! You don't know about it? A whole bunch of kids are going down to the Lake Wannalotta after school tomorrow."

"Who set this up?" Madison asked.

"Me and Chet. Didn't we tell you?" Egg replied.

"No." Madison rolled her eyes. "Anyway, I don't see what the big deal is with skating."

"What planet are you from?" Egg asked. "Skating is *way* cool."

"My cousin used to be a hockey skating champion at his old middle school," Drew said. "That was definitely way cool."

"Your cousin?" Madison asked. "You mean Hart?"

Drew nodded.

"So . . . is Hart going to be skating, then, too?" Madison asked.

"Of course, Maddie," Egg cracked. "Everyone is going. You can't miss it."

Madison looked down at her desk and sucked in her breath. She didn't know how to skate very well, a fact that never seemed to matter before, but now it mattered a lot. She chewed on the inside of her lip and thought about her options. Could she just skip the whole skating scene without attracting too much attention? And while she was at it . . . wasn't there a way she could get out of her math test, too?

Egg leaned over and pinched her shoulder before returning to his seat. "You'd better be there," he said. "Or I'll never let you forget it."

Madison just nodded and tried to smile.

Chapter 2

"So, are you ready for your math test?" Aimee asked Madison as they walked home from school that day.

Madison stuck out her tongue like she'd eaten something yucky. "No. Math is my enemy. Do you think I can get out of the test somehow?"

Aimee laughed as she retied her purple wool scarf around her neck. "Yeah, sure. And while you're at it, why don't you get out of your English paper and all your other homework, too? And why don't you find world peace? And then why don't you find a cure for—"

"Ha, ha! Very funny, Aim," Madison said, crinkling her nose with disapproval. As much as Madison loved her BFF, she hated the sarcasm that often came along with Aimee.

Aimee just giggled. "Race ya!" she said, and took off down the block.

The pair ran the shortcut route, dashing through someone's backyard and down a side street. Then they skipped over to Blueberry Street, where they'd both lived since they were babies. The girls were breathless from running in the cold, cold air.

"So, you didn't tell me, what are you wearing to the skating party tomorrow?" Aimee asked, still huffing a little.

Madison frowned. "What do you mean, *party*?"

"No, no, I don't mean party like *that*. I mean . . . well, you know. I'm wearing my lemon-drop ski parka, and I have these great new jeans with embroidery up the sides. I think I might even wear my—"

"Oh," Madison interrupted. "What is a person supposed to wear to a skating thing?"

"What's the matter with you, Maddie?" Aimee asked.

Madison shrugged. "Whatever."

Aimee came to a complete stop. "Something is totally the matter, isn't it? I can tell these things."

"What?" Madison said.

Sometimes best friends could be annoying even when they were trying to help out the most. Aimee was ultrapersistent.

"I have an excellent idea. Why don't you borrow my Fair Isle sweater for skating tomorrow? It was my mom's, and she is a wicked good ice-skater."

"I don't need your mom's sweater, Aim," Madison said. She sighed. "What I need is to learn how to skate."

"You can skate! I remember last year, you—"

"—sat on the side of the ice and clapped for everyone else," Madison finished Aimee's sentence.

"Oh. Yeah." Aimee frowned.

"And the year before that, I pretended I had a sprained ankle. Remember?"

"You mean to tell me it wasn't sprained?" Aimee said.

Madison chuckled. "Aim, it was *your* idea to make up that excuse."

"Oh yeah," Aimee said. "Gee, it was so good, I fell for it."

"Look, I gotta run home," Madison said, smiling her widest smile. She leaned in and hugged her friend. "And I'll probably go to the skating thing, so don't worry."

"Promise me you will go," Aimee demanded, sticking out her pinky for a pinky swear. *"Promise."*

Madison pulled off her green wool gloves to squeeze.

"Hey, Aim, are you gonna call Fiona?" Madison asked before they said their last good-byes. "I wonder if she's feeling any better."

"I'm going to go call her right now. Why don't you go home and we can all go online together?"

"That's a great idea," Madison said. She turned toward her house.

"And don't forget your other promise!" Aimee yelled after her.

Madison tossed her head as if to say, "No problem," but inside, she was feeling bad already about the pinky swear. Madison had a sinking feeling she might have to break her promise to Aimee.

As soon as she'd dumped her book bag in the front hallway, Madison said hello to Mom and her cute pug, Phin, who were in the kitchen. Then she bounded upstairs to her bedroom and pulled on her favorite new woolly sock-slippers with monkeys woven on top, the ones Mom gave her for Christmas. When it was this cold outside, Madison liked nothing better than getting as snuggly as she could as soon as she arrived home.

Lying across the bed on her tummy, Madison booted up her computer. She opened a brand-new file.

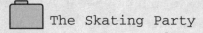 The Skating Party

Once Mom and I watched this movie called
Ice Castles on TV. It was really old, and
it was about a girl and guy who were
professional skaters and then they fell
in love. Even though it was from the
seventies, I loved that movie soooo much.
I wish that could be me, like me and Hart

skating together. Something about that
makes my stomach all fluttery.

    Rude Awakening: Is it a real problem to
go ice skating with someone who makes you
melt?

After writing a few more pages, Madison closed
the file on skating—for the time being. But she was
still obsessing about the skating. Should she go . . .
or not?

What would Bigwheels do?

Madison plugged in her supersecret online pass-
word and logged on to bigfishbowl.com to see if her
keypal Bigwheels was online. She probably wouldn't
be, since she lived in Washington State, which was
all the way across the country. It was three hours
earlier in Bigwheels's world at that very moment,
which meant Bigwheels was in school instead. But
Madison decided e-mail was better than no conversation at all.

From: MadFinn
To: Bigwheels
Subject: Ice-Skating Trauma
Date: Mon 15 Jan 4:03 PM
_____

How is school?

Okay, so I have a very important
question for you: Have you ever
fallen while skating?

Well, I have. On my face,
practically, so ice went up my
nose. And I almost cut my hand on
the blade of an ice skate, too, and
that freaked out my dad. This was
all when I was six or something.
Since then the whole idea of
SKATING freaks me a little bit.

So my dilemma is this skating
thing, and you-know-who will be
there. Should I go and risk
mortification (is that a real
word?). Or should I stay at home
with my dog, Phin, where it's
supersafe? (You know my vote.)

I wish you were online so you could
write back now.

Yours till the ice breakers,

MadFinn

**No sooner had Madison hit SEND than she got an
Insta-Message.**
It wasn't Bigwheels, though. It was Aimee.

<BalletGrl>: So I called Fiona and
    she's soooo sick
<MadFinn>: Oh no

<BalletGrl>: She has a fever of like 102
<MadFinn>: :-(
<BalletGrl>: I talked to Chet & her mom
<MadFinn>: Is she going 2 school tomorrow?
<BalletGrl>: NO & she can't go sk8ing either
<MadFinn>: Is skating off then?
<BalletGrl>: (@@)
<MadFinn>: Yeah HHOK
<BalletGrl>: U r gonna be AWESOME skating ur such a worrywart
<MadFinn>: Should I call F now
<BalletGrl>: Not tonite she's sleeping her mom said
<MadFinn>: R u studying for math now
<BalletGrl>: I don't have a test YOU do . . . hello I only said that 2 u like a million times
<MadFinn>: Oops :-(
<BalletGrl>: W-E
<MadFinn>: Do u have dance class Tues?
<BalletGrl>: yup pointe 2 hrs after school (grrr)
<MadFinn>: C u in the morning?
<BalletGrl>: Let's walk 2 school. Bye!
MadFinn: TTFN

Madison turned off her computer just in time to hear Mom call her downstairs for dinner. They were having vegetarian soufflé, only it had "fallen" while inside the oven.

"Is it supposed to look so flat?" Madison asked Mom.

"It doesn't look as nice, but it tastes exactly the same," Mom said, rushing to serve it before it got any flatter.

Madison picked out all the peppers in her piece and took a bite. Surprisingly, the soufflé wasn't that bad tasting at all. Mom's cooking was definitely improving. Since the big D (as in divorce), Mom was trying much harder to be a better chef, a better housekeeper, and a much better organizer.

"So how was school today?" Mom asked.

Madison took another bite and just shook her head. "Mmmmfffine," she mumbled.

"Walter called here earlier, you know. I think you must have been on the computer."

"Egg called?" Madison asked.

"Yes, he told me to remind you to bring your ice skates to school. What's that all about? Since when do you like ice skating?" Mom said.

Madison wanted to scream, but she calmly replied, "I don't."

"So why are you going skating?" Mom asked.

"Just forget it, Mom," Madison answered. "Please."

Mom sat back in her kitchen chair and took a

sip of her water. "What's going on, Madison?" she said.

"Huh? Nothing's going on, Mom. Some kids are going skating and asked me to come. What are you smiling at?"

"You make me smile," Mom said quietly.

Madison shook her head. "What's the point of going when I can't skate?"

"Oh, honey bear, you can skate. You can do anything you set your—"

"You just don't understand, Mom," Madison pleaded. "You just don't."

"Well, maybe not," Mom said. "But I was only trying to help."

Madison's heart sank. She could tell that her mom was annoyed. This week they'd already had a few big arguments.

Just yesterday, Dad had called from Denver, where he was visiting on a business trip. He wasn't sure if he was coming back in time for his weekly dinner for Madison. Mom didn't like hearing about that. It upset her that Dad would extend a trip to Denver with his new girlfriend, Stephanie—and change plans on Madison. To make matters worse, Madison defended *Dad*.

Big mistake.

Brrrrrrrrrrring.

Mom reached across the kitchen counter to pick up the phone.

"Oh, how are you, Mother?" Mom said, pretending to be chipper. Mom's mom, Gramma Helen, was on the line. "What's new? Oh? Well, nothing much. No, we weren't watching TV. We were just finishing our dinner. Oh? Well, Maddie's right here. Let me get her."

Mom covered the receiver and whispered to Madison, "She's talking a mile a minute. You talk to her."

"Gramma?" Madison squealed when she took the phone.

Gramma squealed right back. She explained how she'd been watching the Weather Channel like she always did from six to six-thirty on weeknights, when she saw something particularly peculiar on the travel report.

"There's a great big mess of a snowstorm headed right for Far Hills!" Gramma exclaimed. "They said the name of the town and everything right there on the TV, would you believe it?"

Madison gasped. "A snowstorm?"

With phone in hand, she wandered over to the bay window in the living room, pressed her warm nose onto the cold window, and looked outside. All she could see were shadows on the porch from streetlights. No snow yet.

"Are you *sure*, Gramma?" Madison asked.

Mom called out from the other room. "She's right! The Weather Channel has a special warning for our area."

After Madison said good-bye to Gramma, she made a secret, secret wish.

"I hope we have a super-snow day tomorrow," she said to herself. "Like the biggest snowstorm ever."

Madison imagined giant white snowdrifts everywhere, with snow that kept falling even when she begged it to stop. No one would be able to go anywhere or do anything.

No school . . .

No math test . . .

And most important . . .

NO skating.

Chapter 3

Brrring! Brrring! Brrring!

Madison opened her eyes. It was so dark.

She couldn't feel her feet because they were buried down under the blankets on her bed. Her entire body was wrapped in the comforter like a mummy, so it took effort to roll over to see her alarm clock. It was 6 A.M.

Phin, who had been nestled on the floor inside the folds of an old blanket, jumped up on the bed. Madison heard her mom talking on the phone but didn't hear exactly what she was saying.

Only the teeniest peek of light was coming in around the edges of her curtains. It was between night and morning, that just-before-dawn time when anything could happen.

"Madison?" Mom whispered from the doorway.

Madison's eyes snapped shut. She pretended to still be asleep.

"Madison?" Mom said, a little louder this time. "I know you can hear me. That was the PTA phone chain. School is canceled today. There's more than a foot of snow on the ground."

"Mo-om?" Madison's voice croaked. Her body tingled. She'd wished for a snow day, and now here it was.

Mom walked over to the bed and sat on the edge. A little more light was beginning to sneak in through the curtains, so Madison could see the soft outline of Mom's face. She was smiling.

"Why don't you sleep in for a little while, honey bear?" Mom said, tucking her in even tighter than before. "Sleep in, and when you get up, we'll make waffles."

Phin was walking around on the bed, with his curlicue tail in motion.

"Yum, waffles," Madison said softly.

Mom kissed the top of her head and grabbed Phin, who was getting frisky like he wanted to go out. "I'm going to walk Phin before it gets any snowier. You close your eyes and go back to dreaming, Maddie."

Unfortunately, the last thing Madison could do right now was sleep. As soon as Mom disappeared with Phin, Madison wriggled out of her mummy wrap and began tossing. The light was getting brighter and brighter because outside was getting whiter and whiter.

Madison jumped up and ran to the window.

Wow!

While she was sleeping, someone had dumped powdered sugar all over the neighborhood—or at least that's what it looked like. No one from the city had plowed or driven on the street yet, so every patch of pavement was covered in white. And snow was still falling.

"Mooooooom!" Madison yelped as she tugged on her jeans and socks. She pulled them on right under her Lisa Simpson nightshirt and then threw a sweater on over that. "Mooooom!"

But Mom didn't answer. She was outside with Phinnie.

Madison went into the back hallway to get her winter snow boots and laced them up tight, put on her green gloves and jacket, wrapped a scarf around her nose and mouth, tugged on her rainbow-striped woolen cap, and opened the front door.

Madison could see one set of people prints (Mom's) and another set of pooch prints (Phin's) going down the path toward the street.

"Mom? Phinnie?" Madison called out. Her voice echoed in the still morning air.

"Quiet, Maddie! Everyone can hear you!" Mom shushed her from up the street, hustling back home. She let go of the leash, and Phin ran as fast as his chubby little body would take him, all the way to Madison.

They wandered around outside for a little while longer, skidding across the soft snow. Madison brushed clumps of white off the tops of bushes. The snow was too soft to make snowballs. It disintegrated in her hands like flour.

Around the neighborhood, people had begun to wake up. Madison could see yellow lights burning in a few windows. The retired fireman who lived across the street was already up, shoveling his driveway. Way off in the distance, Madison could hear the vroom of a plow making its rounds. Soon the powdery street snow would be packed up against the curb.

"I can't believe we don't have school!" Madison said, grinning from ear to ear. She rubbed the bottoms of Phin's paws, which were icy and wet. He was shivering.

"We should go inside," Mom suggested.

Madison followed her up to the house. Along the way, she saw a row of icicles on their porch post and pulled one off. Clutching the icicle made her remember. Sucking on ice was something she used to do all the time in second grade, when she and Ivy Daly were best friends.

Second grade.

That time seemed so long ago from right now.

Madison moved an icicle into her mouth carefully so it wouldn't stick to her lip. She remembered how Ivy once put two small icicles on her lips, letting them stick there and pretending to be a walrus.

Ivy used to be so good at making Madison laugh.

It's a bad storm, folks.
Yes, indeed, up to two feet inland and a foot along the coast.
And we're not done yet!
Expect more snow this afternoon.

Madison flipped the channels to see what other stations were saying about the weather. She couldn't believe this snowstorm had dropped so much snow—and wasn't over yet.

"It's cold out there!" Mom said, moving the boots from a slushy puddle in the hall to the porch. "Let's make some cocoa, too."

"Mmm—yummy," Madison said, nodding. She went to the cupboard and got the hot chocolate and the waffle mix. "Mom, it's almost eight. Do you think it's too early to call Aimee?"

"Not at all. Her father is probably over at the bookstore already," Mom said. She was talking about Book Web, a bookstore and cybercafé that Aimee's parents owned in downtown Far Hills.

Madison dialed, but the Gillespie line was busy.

She tried Fiona's house next, but Mrs. Waters answered and said her daughter was still sleeping. "May I please leave a message?" Madison asked sweetly. Mrs. Waters said Fiona would call as soon as she woke up.

Madison dialed Aimee's house for a second time. It was still busy.

There was a chance that Aimee was online, so Madison dashed upstairs to get her laptop computer. She'd get in touch with her BFF somehow. Madison plugged in the phone jack and dialed up the bigfishbowl.com Web site.

The home page was *swimming* with members.

```
Hotstuff76
Jessica_01
Qtpiegal2
BryanSarah
Peacenluv11
BalletGrl
```

Aimee *was* there! For someone who had only just learned about using computers, Aimee was on the Web more than anyone else Madison knew.

Madison sent a surprise Insta-Message to her friend.

```
<MadFinn>: Hiya!!!
<BalletGrl>: Hi!
<MadFinn>: Can you believe all this
    snowwww?
<BalletGrl>: :^D
<MadFinn>: Soooo whassup?
```

29

```
<BalletGrl>: I have to do shoveling
   with my brothers and then Dad
   asked us all to help @ the store
<MadFinn>: So you can't hang out
<BalletGrl>: Sorry I can't right
   now. Plus my dance lesson was
   canceled, which is a real bummer
<MadFinn>: Is anyone else doing
   stuff
<BalletGrl>: I don't know
<MadFinn>: I know Fiona is still in
   bed:-~(
<BalletGrl>: What r u doing
<MadFinn>: 0 (like the big goose
   egg)
<BalletGrl>: Come to the store then
   w/us
<MadFinn>: Hmmmmm
<BalletGrl>: Well call me there L8R
   then, promise?
<MadFinn>: Ok ok
<BalletGrl>: Gotta run
<BalletGrl>: *poof*
```

After Madison signed out of the conversation, she returned to the home page to check her e-mail. But before she could even select the MAIL key, she was Insta-Messaged again.

```
<Wetwinz>: Hi Maddie
<MadFinn>: Hi Fiona
```

```
<Wetwinz>: I am soooo sick
<MadFinn>: Y r u on the computer I
    thought you were still in bed
<Wetwinz>: My mom doesn't know I'm
    up
<MadFinn>: Whats wrong w/u?
<Wetwinz>: Fever, chills, puking it
    is gross Mom says I have to stay
    in bed until it goes away and I
    have a headache too I'm supposed
    to be under the covers now
<MadFinn>: :>(
<Wetwinz>: Where's Aim today
<MadFinn>: cybercafé
<Wetwinz>: DLTM
<MadFinn>: Yup she's working can u
    believe it
<Wetwinz>: Bummer for a snow day
<MadFinn>: Bigger bummer = being
    sick = you
<Wetwinz>: I'd say come over but I
    don't wanna breathe on you and my
    mom won't let me go out
<MadFinn>: Oh well
<Wetwinz>: 911 my mom is coming
<MadFinn>: Call me 18r
```

Madison saw that she had mail. Maybe she had a note back from Bigwheels.

Bigwheels hadn't written, but there *was* e-mail from Dad.

```
From: JeffFinn
To: MadFinn
Subject: SNOW
Date: Tues 16 Jan 7:11 AM
```

What do you get when you cross
Dracula with the snowstorm in Far
Hills? Frostbite!

Hey, sweetheart, I'm here in Denver
with Stephanie. Oh, boy, there's so
much snow there and here, I can't
even get a flight out until tomorrow.
How is it there? How is Phinnie?
He always hated walking in the
snow because his feet got
frozen.

Needless to say, I'm stuck here in
Colorado. I will try to call or
e-mail later on today. As soon as
I get back, I'm taking you out for
dinner and a movie, too. How does
that sound? Write back to me.

Love,
Dad

Madison was a little sad about Dad's not being able to see her this week, but the joy of the lucky snow day was taking over.

Nothing could get her down today. Madison was free as a bird. She'd watch a video for starters. Then she'd catch up with her friends later.

"Maddie?" Mom called to her from the other room.

Madison bit her lip. Something in the tone of Mom's voice told her that she wouldn't want to hear what Mom had to say.

"Maddie," Mom said again, appearing at the bedroom door. "There you are! I've been calling you for five minutes."

"I was online," Madison mumbled.

"Well, I got this terrific idea and I need your help."

There was that word Madison dreaded most: *Help.*

"Help for what, Mom?" Madison asked cautiously.

Mom chuckled. "It's nothing bad, so you can get that look off your face. I think it'll be fun. I want you to come up to the attic with me and look around in the old boxes. I need some backup materials for the documentary I'm working on. I can't find some of the paperwork, and I'm sure it's up there."

Madison buried her face into a pillow on her bed and then lifted her head up quickly again. "Help go through boxes? Today?" Madison asked.

Mom crossed her arms and smiled. "Today," she said simply.

Madison knew what that meant.

No escape.

Chapter 4

"When was the last time you were up here?" Madison asked as they entered the attic. It smelled like wet carpet from when there had been a leak last summer.

"Oh, I don't know. I brought up all those cartons that had been sitting in my office. Those over there."

Mom pointed to a few boxes with yellow labels that read BUDGE FILMS, the name of Mom's production company.

"Then what are all *these*?" Madison asked.

She pointed to a mountain of other boxes in all shapes and sizes that were pushed up against one wall. Some were ripped on the sides, and others were covered in dust. No one had touched most of these boxes in years. In the middle of the floor was a half-open box with tinsel coming out. It was their

Christmas ornament box. Mom still hadn't put away all the decorations.

"You know, Fiona's attic isn't this messy, Mom," Madison said.

"Well, Fiona just moved here from California. We've been here for a little while longer."

"I guess," Madison said, shrugging. She looked around some more.

On one wall of the attic, the sun glimmered in through a round window. One of the coolest-looking parts of the house was the attic window. Madison had never really noticed how beautiful it looked until just now.

"So what are we supposed to do?" Madison asked her mother.

"Look for my papers—and whatever else we may find. Our lives are up here, packed in boxes. It's amazing, isn't it?" Mom said, resting her elbow on the corner of an old dresser.

"Hey!" Madison said. She spied the gleam of a lock and pressed her body between two boxes to lift out an old case. "What's this?"

"That must be my old flute," Mom said, taking it from her. "I thought that was thrown out ages ago."

Madison had been playing the flute on and off throughout elementary school. She'd nearly given it up since junior high began and she found herself busier than busy with other work. She hadn't realized that Mom played the flute, too.

"I never knew you played! Can you still play?" Madison asked enthusiastically.

"Oh no!" Mom giggled. "Your father tried to get me started up again a few times when we were first married, but . . ."

Mom stopped midsentence. The phone was ringing downstairs.

"I have to grab that!" Mom said, moving to the attic stairs. "It's my office. You dig around and tell me what else you find up here. I'll probably be a little while if it's my editor on the phone."

"Okay, see ya," Madison said, still holding the dusty flute case. She opened it up and peered inside. The flute had tarnished. It felt cold to the touch. Inside the case, she also found a piece of old sheet music for a song by the Beatles. Madison set the case, flute, and music aside.

She didn't know where to look next. Suddenly the drudgery of an attic "job" seemed exciting to Madison. This was like a magical treasure hunt.

One box read TAX DOCUMENTS. Madison moved that out of the way. Behind it, there was a wooden box with an old phonograph player inside. The lining of the box was moth-eaten, and the player didn't look like it worked, but Madison cranked the handle to see what would happen. Dust flew everywhere. A very thick record turned around and around, but no noise came out.

"No wonder they invented CDs," Madison said, moving to another space in the attic.

There was a shelf of books up against the wall, too. She hadn't seen it at first when she walked inside. The dim light from the round window made it hard to see. Madison saw rows of titles on botany, birds, law, and everything else she could imagine. The covers were dust covered, though, so Madison could barely read the gilded titles.

There was an entire row of books by Louis L'Amour, a western author Madison's grampa Joe had loved to read, before he died. Madison pulled one book off a shelf to see the pages inside. The binding cracked as she opened the book. There was an inscription: *To Joe with all my heart, Helen.*

Madison smiled at the idea of Gramma Helen and Grampa Joe being together, in love. She wished love could last forever and ever. But sometimes it didn't. She knew that now.

Madison wondered if her love for Hart Jones would last forever—or at least as long as seventh grade lasted.

"Madison!" Mom yelled up to her.

Madison rushed over to the attic stairs. *"What?"*

"Honey bear, get down here quick. I just put on the weather, and it says we're supposed to get more snow." Mom was talking frantically. She always made fun when Gramma Helen talked that way, but the truth was that Mom talked faster than fast most of the time.

37

She told Mom she'd be right down, then she went back to lock up the new-old flute. On her way back out, Madison tripped over a box that was marked BRAZIL, FILMING—NEW. It had a Budge Films yellow label, too.

"Hey, Mom, I think I found your office stuff here," Madison said.

"Okay," Mom yelled back. "Then we'll get it after lunch. You have to come down and see this weather report, though. We've got some kind of cold front headed our way. Wowza. Their map of the United States is covered in clouds."

As Madison entered the kitchen, she could tell Mom was making grilled cheese sandwiches. The kitchen smelled like burned toast.

"We should go get some supplies," Mom said, eyes on the small television set in the kitchen.

"Supplies?" Madison asked. "Are you worried we're going to be buried in snow or something?"

"You never know, and it is definitely—"

"Better to be safe than sorry," Madison interrupted. "That's what Gramma always says."

"So eat up your sandwich and we'll go to the store," Mom said. She disappeared upstairs to put on different clothes and makeup. She usually had to "put on her face" before heading out.

Madison turned the volume back up on the weather alert that the local news show kept replaying. MAJOR STORM WARNING kept scrolling across the bottom of the TV screen. *This was serious.*

As she took a chewy bite of her grilled cheese, Madison once again reflected on the events of the past day.

She had wished for a snowstorm, and a snowstorm had been provided. Now another snowstorm was coming.

Did Madison wish one time too many?

Once again the phone rang. Madison jumped up to answer, which was good since it was a call for her. Aimee was calling from Book Web.

"Oh my God, it is sooooo busy here," Aimee blurted. "No wonder Daddy wanted some help. Even with my brothers and me we're busy. You should really come down and see—"

Aimee hadn't even given Madison a chance to say hello before she started to talk . . . and talk . . . and talk. She did that a lot.

Finally she asked how Madison was doing.

"I'm okay, I guess," Madison replied. "I'm helping my mom out, too, with her work."

"Cool!" Aimee said. "Can you believe all the snow we got? I'm sorry we can't hang out. Maybe later?"

"The weather lady says that there's more on the way," Madison said.

"More?" Aimee yelled, so loudly, Madison had to pull the receiver away from her ear. "Did you say *more*?"

"Yes," Madison said. "And would you stop screeching, please?"

They both laughed.

"The only bad part is that the whole skating thing is canceled," Aimee said. She sighed. "They closed the whole area by the lake because someone drove their car into a ditch near there. That's what my brother Roger said."

"Oh no . . . really?" Madison feigned disappointment. But she could feel her body *hum*. She didn't mind if skating was canceled! That was what she'd been hoping! She tried to mask her excitement, to keep her truer-than-true feelings hidden from everyone else, even her best friend.

But it was hard to fake out her best friend. Aimee already knew the truth.

"Don't act all sad, Maddie! I know you didn't want to go to the lake," Aimee said. "You don't have to pretend like you're bummed out or anything. I know how you feel about skating."

"You . . . *what*?" Madison was embarrassed, but she grinned so wide, Aimee could probably *hear* the grin through the phone line. "You do?"

"Yeah, I do," Aimee said. "And it's okay."

Madison felt so relieved.

No skating—and no secrets from her best friend, either.

Someone asked Aimee to help out in the bookstore, so she had to get off the telephone, but it

40

turned out to be good timing because at that *exact moment* Mom came downstairs.

"Let's hit the road!" she said.

Madison grabbed her rainbow hat and green gloves.

The roads were busier than they'd been earlier that morning, but there were still fewer cars than on a nonsnowy, ordinary day. Mom drove slowly so the car wouldn't slip and slide all over the wet, slushy streets. By the time they pulled into the parking lot near the Far Hills Shoppes, the wind had picked up a little. The sky turned ashen white, like all the color had been sucked right out.

They stopped in at the Tool Box hardware store first. Mom picked up a box of extra-large candles, three new flashlights and extra batteries, and a new shovel. Their old shovel had gotten a big dent in it when Mom tried shoveling that morning and hit a slab of ice.

Afterward they circled over to Stationery Barn, an office-supply outlet. Mom was a sucker for gold paper clips and neon-colored pens. She loved jazzy office accessories so much that whenever she took Madison shopping, they came home with armfuls of notebooks and files and folders they didn't need. Today Mom used "cleaning out the attic boxes" as her excuse to buy new cartons, folders, and special labels for the folders. Madison benefited from the shopping spree. She got a cool pen with a squishy-soft, orange gel grip.

The shops were bustling. Everyone was either standing in line for caffè latte at The Coffee Mill or buying supplies for the storm that was coming their way. All anyone could talk about was the weather. Madison began to fear the worst. What if they were covered with fifteen feet of snow and frozen for an eternity until some future civilization dug them out of the ice?

Across the mall, Madison thought she spied Poison Ivy and Rose Thorn, shopping for clothes, but they disappeared before Madison could find out for sure. She bumped into Dan Ginsburg for real, however. He was looking over the stand that sold baseball hats. Madison was friends with Dan from seventh grade and from the Far Hills Animal Shelter, where she was a volunteer.

"Hey, Maddie!" Dan said, giving her a high five. He was always in a good mood. "My mom was just talking about you this morning. She wants to know if you're coming in next week for the massive winter cleaning."

Dan's mom, Eileen, was a nurse at the animal clinic.

"Yeah, sure, I'm all for cleaning," Madison giggled. "My mom has me cleaning junk out of the attic today."

"Sorry for you!" Dan said.

"Actually, I'm the one who's sorry, Dan. I haven't been around that much. How are all the animals?"

Madison had begun her volunteer stint at the clinic by going three times a week, but now she only went once every other week. She wanted very much to get back to more regular visits.

"Maddie, the animals miss you. And that dachshund you liked was adopted, by the way. Did I tell you that?" Dan asked.

Madison had grown attached to many dogs at the clinic, including a miniature dachshund named Rosebud. Now Rosebud had found a new family. Madison felt so happy about that. She wanted all the dogs to find happy homes.

"Any *new* animals?" she asked Dan.

He nodded. They were now boarding a runaway golden retriever, a scruffy beagle, two parrots, and a litter of tabby kittens. He said they'd also fixed up a German shepherd that had gotten hit by a car.

Madison turned away for just a moment to see her mother walking toward them. She waved and wrapped up the conversation with Dan.

It was time to head home again through the snow and ice. One stop at the supermarket for food and they'd be fully armed and ready for the arrival of the next storm.

Later that afternoon, Madison had helped Mom shovel the front steps and sidewalk, and had taken Phin for a stroll around the block. But she felt lost without her friends. Aimee was at the bookstore.

Fiona was sick. No one else had called. Not even Egg.

To fight the boredom, Mom suggested she head back up to the attic, but Madison didn't feel like it anymore. She turned on her laptop instead.

She plugged in the Web site address for the Weather Channel from TV and saw more maps showing snow and clouds and other storm signs. Then she surfed over to bigfishbowl.com, but the server was down, and she couldn't get into any of the chat rooms. She also couldn't access "Ask the Blowfish," a special feature on the site that let members ask questions about life, love, and other junk.

Luckily she didn't log off, however. A moment after she'd read the SERVER UNAVAILABLE message for bigfishbowl.com, Madison's Insta-Message icon flashed.

```
<Eggaway>: Yo, Madfinn!
<MadFinn>: Hey Egg whassup
<Eggaway>: Skymoonsunstars
<MadFinn>: VF
<Eggaway>: We're all meeting 18r @
    the lake
<MadFinn>: Isn't that closed?
<Eggaway>: No whats ur prob? I
    wanna sk8! My new hockey sk8s are
    the best
<MadFinn>: (:>|
<Eggaway>: VVF
```

<MadFinn>: When?

<Eggaway>: Like 3 @ the lake

<MadFinn>: I have to get a ride

<Eggaway>: ASK UR MOM

<MadFinn>: Don't yell @ me she's
    working

<Eggaway>: Yo! Maybe Chet's dad can
    drive u

<MadFinn>: Maybe. who's going?

<Eggaway>: Me, Drew, Chet, Hart,
    these other kids Lance and Suresh

<MadFinn>: That's all guys, Egg

<Eggaway>: So?

<MadFinn>: I dunno

<Eggaway>: I think Ivy and Joanie
    may come

<MadFinn>: Oh

<Eggaway>: Hart invited them and
    some other girl who lives next
    door to him, she does real
    skating contests

<MadFinn>: Oh

<Eggaway>: And if it snows today
    again we'll do it later I'll
    e-mail bye!

<MadFinn>: Oh

Madison's heart skipped a beat as she clicked offline.

She immediately opened a new page in one of her existing files.

Hart

Rude Awakening: I keep getting cold feet when it comes to Hart. And it's not because I'm standing in the snow.

It's her.

No matter when, where, or what the situation, everyone notices Poison Ivy. And I just know that this afternoon, Hart will be hanging out with her. I feel like it would be torture to go there and see that happen without Aimee or Fiona to back me up. Even though they still don't know about my crush . . . help!

I wish Bigwheels would write back.

Maybe the guys will be too busy skating to notice? Maybe they'll all play hockey and leave her out? I wish.

Madison glanced away from the computer for a moment to collect her thoughts. From where she was sitting in her bedroom, she had a full view of the window looking out on the street. Some kids were sledding on a slope in her neighbors' yard.

She noticed something. Big fat flakes were just starting to fall again onto the windowsill and glass pane.

More snow. *Already!*

Madison smiled to herself. No one would be meeting at three o'clock today . . . and maybe not even tomorrow. She had an extra day or two to prepare herself for skating, Hart, and Ivy.

The second storm was moving in.

Seventh-grade snow days were about to get *really* interesting.

Chapter 5

"Rowrrooooo!" Phin was standing on Madison's stomach, panting. The clock next to her bed said 8:23 A.M.

Madison leaped out from under the covers and ran to the window. The blanket of snow across Far Hills was at least a foot deeper than the day before—and it was still snowing, snowing, snowing.

She donned her monkey slippers and shuffled down the stairs to breakfast. The smell of pancakes filled the air.

Mom had made a superbatch of silver-dollar cakes. She'd even warmed up syrup in the microwave. Madison felt special. The last time Mom ever did that was for Dad when they were still married. She put fruit slices on top of one pancake for the face: strawberry eyes, banana nose, and orange mouth.

"Mom, you haven't made me smiley pancakes since I was little," Madison said, taking her first enormous bite. "These are so yummy."

Mom sat down at the table. "Isn't this fun, the two of us stuck indoors?"

"Do you think it will ever stop snowing?" Madison asked, taking another big bite of breakfast.

"Doesn't look like it," Mom said, gazing out the kitchen window. "I'm going to get lots of film editing done today, that's for sure. I remember when we had bad storms like this in Chicago, growing up."

The house rattled with the wind.

"Just like that." Mom laughed. "Windy, snowy, really miserable. Your grandmother always sent your aunt Angie and me into the yard to make snow angels. Of course Angie usually beaned me with snow*balls* instead."

Mom told a few more weather-related Chicago stories that made Madison laugh.

When Mom was finished telling stories, Madison called Fiona to see how she was feeling. But she sounded hoarse, so Madison could barely hear her.

"I have a fever of a hundred and one," Fiona said. "I'm all clammy."

"That means the fever is going away, though, right?" Madison asked.

"Mom says I can't even get out of bed. I'm so sick of watching television, and I read my English reading through next week's assignments already," Fiona said.

Madison realized she'd been out of school for a day and a half and she hadn't done any homework yet. She'd have to deal with that later.

"Is Aimee still helping her dad at the store?" Fiona whispered.

"Yeah," Madison said. "But she's not working all of today. We were going to hang out. Can we come over to see you?"

"My mother says I'm still too sick to have visitors." Fiona sighed. "I feel like I'm quarantined from the rest of the planet."

"Well, as soon as she says it's okay, we are totally coming over."

"Is everyone out skating and playing in the snow and all that?" Fiona asked. "My stupid brother won't tell me anything."

"Not really," Madison answered. "Not yet, anyway. The lake was closed yesterday. It's been too stormy."

Fiona giggled a little bit. "I really miss you guys."

"I miss you, too," Madison said. She wanted to tell Fiona all the specifics about the skating party and then the cancellation of the skating party and the rescheduling of the skating party . . . but she decided not to tell her anything. She didn't want Fiona to feel any more "out of it" than she already did. Being sick was the worst feeling in the world, especially when your head felt woozy with cough and cold medicine.

After they said their good-byes, Madison called Aimee. Aimee wasn't going to the bookstore after all. They made a date to walk their dogs in the middle of the blizzard. Madison secretly hoped they could make angels in the snow, too. Just like her mom and Aunt Angie had done when they were her age.

Mom was waiting upstairs in the attic to resume the big clean. She'd torn into a few other boxes and recovered many of the papers she'd been looking for yesterday.

"Do you think you could help me organize some of this information on the computer?" Mom asked Madison. "Like, could we put information on a graph chart together?"

Madison wasn't a hundred percent sure about how to make the perfect graph chart, but she was eager for the computer challenge. She knew that even if she got stuck working on it, she could always ask Mrs. Wing for help. Madison wanted to beef up her computer skills over the next few months so by summer she'd be ready once and for all to start up her very own Web page.

"I can help you, Mom," Madison said. "But can we do it later? I was going to walk Phinnie and go over to Aimee's for a little while."

"Sure. Have fun," Mom said. She was sitting cross-legged in a pile of paper that spread all around her like a puddle. Rubber-banded stacks of slides were piled in between her legs. "I really need to hire an assistant to help me archive these materials."

"I'll help, Mom," Madison said again. "Just later, okay?"

Mom beamed. "You look cute this morning, honey bear. Are you wearing those pajamas over to Aimee's or what?"

Madison made a face and then skipped down into her bedroom. She pulled on a new pair of corduroys with patches on the pockets that had been a Christmas present from Dad's girlfriend, Stephanie. Before leaving her room, she decided to log on to her laptop to see if Egg had sent e-mail with more news on when and where the "new" skating party had been planned.

To her surprise, Madison found her e-mailbox bursting with mail.

FROM	SUBJECT
✉ Eggaway	SK8ING!!!!!
✉ Boop-Dee-Doop	Clearance
✉ JeffFinn	Fw: This is SNOW funny
✉ Webmaster@bigfis	Server Down
✉ Bigwheels	Re: Ice-Skating Trauma

Madison read Egg's note first. He had sent it to a lot of people.

From: Eggaway
To: Chet Wetwins; Fiona Wetwinz; Aim
BalletGrl; Rose Rosean16; Ivy
Flowr99; Hart Sk8ingboy; Susie
Peace-peep; Joan JK4ever; Lance
Bossbutt; Suresh Suresh00; Maddie
MadFinn; Dan Dantheman; Drew
W_Wonka7
Subject: SK8ING!!!!!
Date: Wed 17 Jan 10:33 AM

ok sooo this is the deal we're NOT
meeting today b/c Drew sez the lake
is STILL closed from storm and it's
still snowing n e way. My mom calld
school & she thinks they'll close it
Thursday too so let's mt tomorrow
instead @ 3 at the lake. bye!!!!

Madison looked over the list of "to" names on
Egg's e-mail to see who was invited skating and who
wasn't. Unfortunately, she saw Ivy, Rose, and Joan's
e-mail addresses on the list.

But she also saw another e-mail address.

Hart.

Without thinking, Madison selected Sk8ingboy
and added it to her own address book. She figured
it was good to have, just in case she ever needed to
send him e-mail.

Just in case.

Then Madison moved on to the other mail, deleting the Boop-Dee-Doop "special offer" because she knew Mom wouldn't let her get anything, anyway, and deleting the note from bigfishbowl's Webmaster. She knew the server had been down. She didn't need to read about it anymore.

The next message was from Dad, which was very short and sweet.

```
From: JeffFinn
To: MadFinn
Subject: Have You Heard This One?
Date: Wed 17 Jan 12:13 AM
```

```
What do you get when you cross a
witch with a glacier?
A cold spell!

LOL. Thought that was sort of cute.

Miss you, Maddie.

Love,
Dad
```

Dad had told that one at least three or four times already. It was one of his winter "regulars." Luckily the message from Bigwheels wasn't something she'd already heard. Bigwheels had

actually typed the e-mail the day before.

From: Bigwheels
To: MadFinn
Subject: Re: Ice-Skating Trauma
Date: Tues 16 Jan 8:09 PM

School is same as always. My
parents were doing really well
except Dad moved out again for a
temporary separation. Don't ask. I
told my mom I didn't care, but of
course I do.

How do you deal with your parents?

I LOVE SKATING, by the way. I agree
that it can be a little scary. That
sounded so weird that you almost
got cut on a skating blade. But
it's really not so scary on regular
rinks. I used to skate on a lake.
That was way scarier. I remember
those times when I was very little.
I didn't actually skate, but my dad
did, and he carried me. There was
one time the lake ice cracked. Dad
almost fell in.

I can't wait for the Olympics to
start because I want to watch the

ice skaters do triple-Lutz jumps. I think the ice dancing is my favorite part. They all look so romantic dancing on the ice like that, don't you think?

I don't skate now, but I think you should. It really doesn't matter if you fall. Don't worry about your crush, either. He will NOT fall, either, and definitely not for that Ivy girl. She sounds mean. Trust me.

Write back again soon.

Yours till the snow caps,

Bigwheels

Madison looked over at the clock and gasped. It was way later than she thought.

Aimee was waiting.

She closed her computer down quickly (saving the Bigwheels message for further reply), grabbed her coat, and headed out the door.

The weather outside was nippy. More fat snowflakes were falling, and she stuck out her tongue to lick one out of the air. It tasted like ice cream, but that was no surprise to Madison, who had always believed that snowflakes were naturally sweetened. She ran to Aimee's in less than five minutes.

"Where have you been?" Aimee said when she opened her door. She was in her slippers and jeans.

"You're not even dressed?" Madison asked.

Aimee twirled around and got into some ballerina poses. "No, I'm not dressed. But I look pretty good, don't I?"

"Quit posing and *get dressed*!" Madison said, exasperated. "Please?"

Aimee burst into laughter and ran inside. Madison followed her.

It took Aimee only half an hour to get on all her gear, and in no time, she and Madison were stomping around in the Gillespie backyard. A little while later, Aimee's brothers Billy and Dean came out to join them for a game of snow Frisbee.

Ker-splat!

As Madison reached to catch the Frisbee, she lost her footing. She fell hat over boots into a snowdrift.

"Nice one, Maddie." Billy snickered.

Aimee rushed over to help her up out of the snow, but Madison was laughing so hard, she couldn't even stand.

"I—can't—get—aaaaaaah—help!" Madison cried as she bent forward and fell back again.

Aimee started to giggle, too.

"Hey, did you see that?" Dean said, looking up at

57

the sky. He pointed to a cloud. "I swear I just saw a lightning bolt."

"No way," Aimee said, punching him in the side. Her face was flushed pink from running around in the cold air.

Madison finally stood up, patted the snow off her pants and back, and walked over to her friend. "What are you guys looking at?" she asked.

The sky looked ominous, grayer than before. Another bolt of lightning *did* crack against the winter sky. Evening was on its way.

"I've never seen anything like that before," Billy said.

The four stared and stared, as if staring would make another lightning bolt appear. And then, in the middle of all the dark sky, it began to snow once again.

Madison felt wet drops on her eyelashes. She gazed at other snowflakes as they landed on the front of her hand, examining the crystal shapes up close.

"What time is it, Dean?" Madison asked Aimee's brother.

He looked at his digital watch. "Five-oh-six," he said.

Aimee frowned. "You have to go? Already?"

"I have to walk Phinnie!" Madison shook the snow off her green gloves and ran toward home.

Mom was standing on the porch when she got

there, shoveling some of the snow that had col-
lected near the front door.

"Well, look at you, the Snow Queen!" Mom said,
smiling at Madison's approach.

"Very funny, Mom," Madison replied.

"I ordered pizza for dinner tonight," Mom
added. "And Phin has already been for a walk."

"Sounds good," Madison said, heading for the
house.

"And I want you to help me move some of those
boxes in the attic," Mom said. "I discovered a whole
bunch of stuff up there from grade school."

"From *my* grade school?" Madison asked.

"Yes," Mom answered. "Journals, books, even an
old photo album. They're in a box that's half open.
You were so cute back then. . . ."

"What do you mean, 'back then'?" Madison
laughed.

Mom grinned. "You know what I mean, honey
bear."

Madison grinned back and stepped inside the
front hallway. She tugged off the rainbow hat,
which made her hair stick out in a bouquet of static
electricity.

Old photo album?

She couldn't wait to see what Mom was talking
about.

Chapter 6

Madison's clothes were sopping wet from the game of snow Frisbee. She hadn't realized it until she went to remove them and had to *peel* her pants off.

The answering machine in the front hall was blinking twice, which meant two calls. She hit the PLAY key. A tinny-sounding voice echoed in the hall.

Message one.

"Maddie? Maddie, are you there? It's Daddy, still in Denver, sweetheart. We're holed up here in the hotel at the airport, waiting for the next available flight. Only problem is that the airport is closed and looks like it might stay closed for another day or so. I miss you, Maddie. Stephanie says hello. Tell your mother I said hi. I'll call again later when I think you might be—"

Beeeeeeeep. Message two.

"This is Ronnie Dustin at Budge, calling for Fran Finn. Fran, we have a distributor for that Brazil documentary. Give me a call, please, at your earliest convenience. I'm in the LA office."

Madison clicked STOP and then saved the last message. But she deleted the first one, figuring that Mom probably wouldn't need to hear Dad's voice. Her parents were getting along better these days, but Mom still bristled a little bit at the mention of Dad. She tried to be fair, but no matter what Dad ever did to redeem himself, Mom would find something wrong.

None of that mattered to Madison. She loved everything about her dad, even the parts that weren't so perfect, even the horrible jokes. Plus Dad always noticed and complimented Madison on her outfits.

After playing the messages, Madison hopped upstairs to put on sweatpants, her woolly monkey slippers, and an old plaid shirt she'd inherited from Dad. It was so warm.

She turned on her laptop computer and let it warm up, too, before opening another new file.

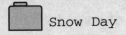 Snow Day

Today was the BEST snow day I have ever had in my entire life, and I am not exaggerating one bit.

Secret admission #1: I maybe have a baby crush on Aimee's brothers again (but only a teeny, tiny one, I swear). They looked soooo cute today outside her house. We played Frisbee for an hour or more, and Aimee was acting kind of dorky, but she always acts weird around her brothers. I don't know why.

Secret admission #2: I think I will go skating at the lake Thursday. I'm getting up my courage. I'm feeling so HAPPY.

I've never seen so much snow in my whole life, like I could get lost in all this snow. Aimee and I made the BEST snow angels, and it was all powdery for perfect wings.

Rude Awakening: Getting left out in the cold can be a good thing. Blizzards are awesome!

While Madison was online, Phinnie came into her room and curled up near her feet. She could feel his warm little pug body. In the next moment, however, he jumped up and scampered up the attic stairs.

"Phinnie?" Madison turned and called after him. "Phinnie, are you there?"

"Rowrrooooooo!" Phin called back. Madison could hear the click-clack-click of his black nails running back and forth in the attic.

She got up quickly to head upstairs, too. Phin would make a huge mess if he started chewing on any of the materials Madison and her mother had left out of boxes.

Madison remembered what Mom had said about the extra items left in one of the open boxes. She took the attic steps by twos and hurried to see what was inside the books and albums.

Once upstairs, Phinnie seemed to calm down. Madison guessed that he'd heard steam in the pipes or a creaking floorboard and gotten jumpy.

The box Mom had mentioned was sitting right by the attic entrance. Madison looked through some of the art projects and pictures. But there was another box that caught Madison's eye.

Madison walked over to the box in the corner of the attic. The box had large red letters that read FRANCINE HOOPER. On top was a rubber-banded pile of old, torn report cards with her Mom's name on them.

The rubber band snapped off in Madison's hand as soon as she reached for it. The cards were chilly from being in storage for so long. Each report card was filled in with so many comments.

Very good writer. Needs improvement on math skills. Suggest extra-credit program for Frannie this summer.

Madison chuckled to herself. Mom had been unsuccessful in math class, too. Just like Madison. Fortunately, summer school hadn't been necessary in Madison's case.

Excellent English papers this term! However, we cannot overlook the fact that Fran needs to get to school on time. Her tardiness has become a problem.

Mom was always late? It seemed funny that Mom would be so angry with Dad for being late when she herself had a problem with lateness on many of the report cards Madison was reading.

Inside the report card box, she discovered newspaper clippings from Mom's school paper, showing Mom taking a jump shot at a basketball game and cramming for finals in a school library.

Next to the report card box, Madison noticed another box marked KEEP OUT! THIS MEANS YOU, MOM AND DAD. Madison recognized the handwriting. She had written it a long time ago. Mom hadn't cracked the seal yet, but Madison did. She found something inside she hadn't seen in years.

Nesting at the top of the box was an old, wooden cigar case covered with decoupage. A long time ago Madison had saved letters, comics, and other special notes in it. Most of the letters and papers had rough edges, torn sides, and broken seals. She'd called this her "secret box."

Opening the box slowly, Madison gasped. She 'd forgotten all this existed! She read and then reread every letter. Her favorite was a note from Gramma Helen, who had written while traveling with Grampa Joe in Europe. Madison had saved the envelope because the stamp was so pretty.

She looked deeper inside the mystery carton to see what else lay buried or wrapped in newspapers beneath the cigar box.

First Madison found a yellow diary with a lock from five years before. It had never been written in. The pages were crackly to the touch.

Then she saw a stack of pictures she'd finger painted in kindergarten. They were mostly painted orange. It had been Madison's favorite color back then, too.

On the bottom of the box, she found a photo album, the one with the word SNAPSHOTS spelled out in big, gold letters across the fake leather album cover. She had gotten the book from Aunt Angie for her eighth birthday.

Madison opened the book very slowly in case there was anything stuffed inside. She didn't want things to fall out. Turning the plastic pages made a lot of noise.

On the first spread of photos, Madison saw herself wrapped in a fuzzy yellow blanket, looking more like a chick than a little baby. There were three poses in that outfit, next to a picture of Madison lying with a bare bottom on the living room floor. She had a big grin on her face and a teddy bear in her hand.

Madison turned the page quickly. Baby pictures could be so embarrassing.

The next spread showed Madison sitting high up on her dad's shoulders. He was standing in the yard, watering flowers. In another photo he was barbecuing hot dogs. That was back when Madison's mom still ate meat. She'd been a strict vegetarian for a few years now.

There was a big photo of Mom and Dad seated together on a hammock. They were kissing, in the picture. Madison stopped to look at that photograph a little longer than the others.

She couldn't take her eyes off her parents. They had looked so happy then. In the photo, Madison could barely make out the shadow of a little child on the left side. She realized she was the one standing just outside the photo's frame. She'd been standing there, watching Mom and Dad kiss.

She glanced through the next few pages to find even more shots of Mom, Dad, herself, and other family members:

Gramma Helen putting Madison's hair into braids.

Grampa Joe carrying Madison into the ocean.

Dad pouring soapy water over Madison's head in the tub.

Mom feeding Madison green mushy food.

Madison jumping on her bed.

Page after page, Madison found the baby and then grade school pictures she'd always loved. She looked through them all twice. And then she got to the pictures of second grade.

There was Ivy Daly. *In almost every single one.*

Their best friendship dated back to the beginning of school. Ivy and Madison had been inseparable. They had dressed alike and liked the same things. They had both liked to blow bubbles, climb trees, and plan tea parties for their dolls.

Madison saw photos that showed all of these things.

She saw an Ivy she'd forgotten existed.

She saw the *nice* Ivy she used to know, once upon a time.

Madison plucked one of her favorite photos off the page, a shot of her and Ivy standing with arms wrapped around each other's shoulders, smiling. She would scan the photo to attach it to her Ivy online file.

At the very end, Madison found the last page stuck to the inside back cover of the photo album. She tried carefully to pry it apart, afraid it would rip.

And no sooner had she peeled it apart than something dropped out.

Something Madison *definitely* was not expecting.

Stuck inside the back cover of the album was a yellowing envelope that Madison barely remembered sealing. The envelope was stained with age-old, dried fingerprints, and someone had marked it very carefully on the outside.

MADISON FINN & IVY DALY
Do Not Open Until Seventh Grade
That Means NO ONE except US!!!

It was an envelope from second grade. Madison

could remember the day when she and Poison Ivy had torn the paper off a legal pad and signed their names in ink. She remembered Ivy hugging her when they licked the envelope shut and added a "backup" seal of black electrical tape, because that was the only tape they could find.

Madison peered closely at the envelope to see what it said. On the back was a different message:

MADISON FINN & IVY DALY
Friends Forever and Ever and Ever
For OUR eyes ONLY!!!

Ivy had drawn teeny little flowers and borders all over the envelope—and every flower Madison saw sent her mind back to the day when the letter had been written.

Madison *always* thought about the fact that Ivy was her mortal enemy. But she rarely thought about why.

Until now.

She picked up the envelope and read it three times more.

Madison could almost hear the sounds from back then, the time when she and Ivy had their seats next to each other in school, when they always teamed up for dodgeball, and when they vowed to *both* win the Far Hills Little Miss pageant together.

Inside the album were taped together pictures

that showed the sides of Ivy most people in junior high had either forgotten or never known: the funny girl, the sometimes-too-shy girl, and even the scared-of-boys girl.

Once upon a time, Ivy hadn't been poisonous.

"Madison!" a voice yelled from downstairs. "What's going on up there? I called for you twice."

Mom had probably reheated pizza and set the table.

"Come on down! Dinner is ready!" she yelled.

"Okay, Mom," Madison mumbled.

Madison placed her secret cigar box back into the dusty carton, putting the report cards, papers, and other life memorabilia on top of that.

"So what time *is* it?" Madison asked as she bounded down the stairs.

Mom said it was six-thirty, and Madison nearly fell over. "Six-thirty? How did it get to be so late?"

"You were obviously having a good time going through boxes, Maddie. You went up there an hour ago," Mom said. "So what did you find?"

Madison could feel the unopened seventh-grade letter from her and Ivy burning a hole inside her pocket . . . but she said nothing.

She would keep *this* discovery to herself—at least for now.

Chapter 7

From: MadFinn
To: Bigwheels
Subject: Need Your Advice
Date: Wed 17 Jan 7:59 PM

Thanks for cheering me up. I won't
worry about Hart if I can help it,
but that's like asking me not to
eat chocolate. I can't!!!

Right now I am worrying about something else instead. I am staring at
this letter on my bed. It's from
Ivy, only it was written like a
million years ago. Well, it was
written by both of us in second
grade. I'm telling you about it

because I just feel so weird having
it. I found it in the attic.

In second grade, Ivy used to be my
best friend on the planet. And we
spent all our time together, mostly
wanting to be as cool as her older
sister, Janet. She was five years
older and she was the coolest. So
when we were in second grade and
Janet was in seventh grade, we
thought that she got to do the best
things. We wrote this list of
things WE wanted to do in seventh
grade—together! And then we signed
it and sealed it and put it away
never to be opened until we were in
the REAL seventh grade.

That's NOW.

What am I supposed to do with this?
I don't like Poison Ivy anymore,
and I don't want to share this
letter with her, because she doesn't
deserve it. But it seems wrong not
to share. Know what I mean? After
all, we did both make a promise,
and we sealed it together. You know
I'm superstitious about things.
Won't I get seven years bad luck or

71

something if I open it on my own?

What do you think? Should I show it
to Ivy? HELP!

As always, I appreciate your advice
from far away.

Write soon.

Yours till the mail boxes,

MadFinn

Madison marked her message to Bigwheels with
a little red exclamation point for priority mail serv-
ice. She wanted to know what to do right away.
All at once, her computer bleeped.
And Bigwheels appeared like some kind of
Internet fairy godmother.

<Bigwheels>: U r online!
   Hellllooooo!
<MadFinn>: Did you get my message?
<Bigwheels>: No what messg?
<MadFinn>:
   Aaaaaaaaaaaaaaaaaaaaaaaaaah
<Bigwheels>: Lemme check now . . .
<Bigwheels>: YES! Ok
<MadFinn>: Hello?
<MadFinn>: Hello?

<MadFinn>: Bigwheels????????

<Bigwheels>: Wait. I wuz reading it

<MadFinn>: SWDYT

<Bigwheels>: (::)(::)

<MadFinn>: Im crankier than cranky
what should I do?

<Bigwheels>: U prob should show the
letter 2 her

<MadFinn>: U think so? Really? Y?

<Bigwheels>: b/c of what u said.
She was part of it and u made a
promise together. I believe in
promises.

<MadFinn>: But she'll probably just
tear it up or laugh in my face

<Bigwheels>: Or not

<MadFinn>: Why r u so optimissic

<MadFinn>: I mean OPTIMISTIC

<Bigwheels>: Just b/c she is mean u
don't have 2 be mean right?

<MadFinn>: I guess how do u know so
much

<Bigwheels>: BTDT

<MadFinn>: Oh

<Bigwheels>: Did u watch the early
skating trials on TV this week?

<MadFinn>: No ur like a sk8ing
fanatic aren't u

<Bigwheels>: Not really I just think
they look so graceful on the ice
I wish I could do that

```
<MadFinn>: Me too I'm Queen of the
   Klutzes I swear
<Bigwheels>: So is it still snowing
<MadFinn>: No
<Bigwheels>: So were you skating
   today too or what?
<MadFinn>: No skating b/c Lake
   Wannalotta is closed
<Bigwheels>: I saw on the weather
   that the snow was moving across
   the country. We're supposed to
   get another storm, too.
<MadFinn>: That's kinda cool so we
   have the same weather
<Bigwheels>: Yes
<MadFinn>: Have u written n e poems
   lately?
<Bigwheels>: Not so much I'm working
   on one what about you?
<MadFinn>: NO!!! I gotta run
<Bigwheels>: Write back soon??
<MadFinn>: Yes! thank u
<Bigwheels>: *poof*
```

**No sooner had Madison exited her Insta-Message
chat with Bigwheels than she got an IM from Fiona.**

```
<Wetwinz>: Maddie?
<MadFinn>: How r u feeling F?
<Wetwinz>: SICK
<MadFinn>: R u taking medicine?
```

<Wetwinz>: Yes, I think I'll be
  better by tomorrow
<MadFinn>: What's tomorrow?
<Wetwinz>: Skating
<MadFinn>: Oh well u r sick maybe
  we'll cancel it
<Wetwinz>: LOL no way Egg would
  never do that
<MadFinn>: It could happen he is
  your CRUSH after all
<Wetwinz>: Double LOL
<MadFinn>: I think he likes u 2
<Wetwinz>: Not right now my nose is
  dripping I feel so gross UGH
<MadFinn>: Thanks for sharing
<Wetwinz>: Maybe you & Aim can come
  over sometime soon
<MadFinn>: Is that ok w/ur mom?
<Wetwinz>: I'll ask her maybe
  tomorrow
<MadFinn>: ?4U did u say Hart came
  over to see Chet?
<Wetwinz>: Yes but I only saw him
  for a minute
<MadFinn>: What were they doing?
<Wetwinz>: Why do u care?
<MadFinn>: I don't I just was
  curious that's all
<Wetwinz>: Ya know, I think Hart is
  kinda cute, too
<MadFinn>: Really

75

<Wetwinz>: Don't you?

Pzzzzzzzzzzzzt!

With a loud, sizzling sound, the power zapped off and Madison's laptop computer screen went black.

"Fiona?" Madison said feebly as she hit a few keys and tried to boot up the laptop again. She was able to get the computer running again on her battery, but the Internet connection was lost.

Power, phones, and all connection to the outside world suddenly ended.

And her room was darker than dark.

It was nine-thirty P.M. and the storm had returned, bringing with it one last gust of wind and wet snow.

Madison felt her way over to the window in her bedroom. Streetlights were out, and all the houses on her block were cloaked in darkness. The only light Madison saw was the faint blue glow of her laptop. It cast a hue and threw shadows on her bedroom wall.

"Maddie?" Mom whispered from Madison's bedroom doorway. She was holding a flashlight. "Where's that blue light coming from?"

"My computer. The battery's still charged," Madison replied.

Mom clicked off her flashlight and came over by the window to put her arms around Madison's shoulders. "This has without a doubt been the worst storm I've ever seen here in Far Hills."

"It's global warming, Mom," Madison said. In addition to caring for endangered animals (and *all* animals), Madison had recently become worried about other environmental issues, too.

"First it snows, then it clears up, then it thunders, then the power goes out. Tomorrow it'll probably be seventy degrees and humid." Mom shook her head.

Madison squeezed Mom's forearm. "Look over there!" she said. "It looks like someone else has a flashlight in their house."

"There, too!" Mom said, pointing.

Madison gazed at her mom's face. Although she looked bluish in the light of the bedroom, Mom still looked so pretty. Madison hadn't really stared at her up close like this in a long time. She was too busy doing homework or something else to notice Mom's eyes or lips or the way Mom's hair curled up top.

"What do you say we go downstairs and light a few of those candles we got at the store today?" Mom suggested.

"Sure," Madison said. "Good thing we bought extra supplies."

Phinnie jumped up on Madison with his two paws and prodded her, whining. He wanted some attention, too.

Mom leaned over and scratched the top of Phin's head.

Phin wheezed. His little brown pug eyes rolled into the back of his head.

"Happy dog." Mom laughed.

They turned on the flashlight again and walked slowly down the stairs toward the living room.

A red-and-blue flashing light zoomed past the front windows.

"Must be the electric company," Mom said.

Mom hummed as she lit a few of the fat, vanilla-scented candles. She arranged them on the coffee table. Then she and Madison sat on the couch together without saying much else.

After a few minutes, Mom took Madison's hair out of its elastics and offered to brush it. Now it was Madison's turn to hum. Mom hadn't brushed her hair in years. It felt so good. After only a few moments of hair brushing, Madison fell asleep.

The next thing Madison remembered was waking up in the well-lit living room, curled up under one of Gramma's quilts. Phinnie was asleep under the coffee table, snoring. It was morning.

"Mom?" Madison said, lifting her head off the couch. She could hear the humming and buzzing of appliances in the kitchen, so she knew the power was back on again.

"You conked right out last night, honey bear," Mom said from the doorway to the kitchen. "I sat there as long as I could, but then my arm fell asleep."

"I don't even remember . . ." Madison said, yawning.

"Well, it's Thursday, so you better get a move on," Mom said. "Looks like the snow really has stopped for good. The sun is out, too. I'm assuming you'll be spending the day with friends?"

"Friends?" Madison repeated. She flipped over on the couch to look out the living room window. It was brighter than bright outside. The storm was long gone. She got a sinking feeling in her stomach. Today would definitely be the day when everyone met at the lake to skate.

Madison stuck her head under the quilt and wished for more snow, more time, more *something*!

But it was too late for wishing.

"Madison?" Mom yelled from the kitchen. "Didn't you hear the phone? Come on and answer it. It's Walter."

"Walter?" Madison moaned. She went over to the phone. "Hi, Egg."

"Hey, Maddie!" Egg yelled into the receiver. "We're meeting at eleven at the lake. Be there!"

"Um, Egg, I'm not sure I can go," Madison said.

"Get out of here," he said. "Everyone is going except for Fiona, and you have to be there. You promised."

Madison sighed. "I can't."

"Yeah, whatever. I'll see you at eleven," Egg said. He hung up.

Madison immediately dialed Aimee's number.

"Help!" she said as soon as Aimee picked up the phone. "What am I gonna wear to the lake?"

Aimee laughed. "Relax, Maddie. I'll be right over."

Chapter 8

"Why don't you want to wear this?" Aimee suggested. "You always liked my striped ski sweater."

"I just don't know. Stripes make me look fat," Madison said.

"What are you talking about?" Aimee said.

"Look at my hair. It's all static electricity. I can't go out like this."

They were standing inside Madison's bedroom with the closet doors thrown open and half of the closet now on the floor.

Aimee stepped over a pile of shirts and bent down to look through them a second time. "It's just a dumb afternoon skate. Let's not get so freaked out about the whole thing."

"I am! I can't *skate*!" Madison said.

"Okay, okay." Aimee backed off.

Madison rifled through the few items that remained on hangers inside the closet. Then she apologized.

"I'm sorry, Aim. I just don't like the idea of falling on my butt in front of everyone from school—including Poison Ivy. She'll use that against me for years."

Aimee nodded. "Well, maybe. But who cares about her? I thought we decided that we didn't care about what Ivy said or did."

"We don't," Madison blurted.

But what she wanted to do was scream.

Madison wanted to tell Aimee about the sealed letter she'd found in the attic, about how she missed the Ivy she knew in second grade, and about how she suddenly felt weirder than weird about being in Ivy's presence.

"Maddie?" Aimee asked. "How about *this* sweater? I've never seen you wear this one."

She held up one of Madison's newest sweaters, a Christmas present from Mom. It was orange angora, fuzzy all over like a tabby cat.

"Maybe," Madison said. She'd never even put it on.

"It's your favorite color, right?" Aimee said. "Go ahead and try it."

Madison slipped it over her head. It fit snugly, but it was so warm and cozy. "I like this one," Madison said, moving over to look in the full-length mirror.

Aimee picked up a pair of jeans from the floor. "And wear it with these, which won't look weird if you fall on the ice. . . . I mean . . ."

Madison glared at Aimee. "If I *fall*? Thanks a lot, Aim! That's like a whammy. Now I'm destined to fall."

"I—I didn't mean to say that," Aimee stammered. She fell backward onto Madison's bed and started to laugh a little. "You are so paranoid, I swear."

Madison slipped on the jeans. "Well, I guess this looks okay," she said to her reflection.

"It looks fab! Now I have to go home and get dressed," Aimee said. "It's already ten o'clock. Everyone's meeting in an hour."

"Can your brother give us a ride over to the lake?" Madison asked.

"Yeah, someone will. I don't know if Roger or Billy is going to Dad's store today. And my mother has a yoga workshop or something. She left this morning."

"Your mom is so busy," Madison said.

"She said you could come for dinner tonight if you want. We're having tofu lasagna."

"Um, no thanks." Madison bit her lip. "I have plans with Mom already."

Madison couldn't stomach even the idea of eating another all-natural, nut-and-grains-and-tofu meal at Aimee's place. She loved squirrels, but she didn't see the point in eating like one. Besides,

Mom's "scary dinners" of fast food had been fast improving, so eating at home wasn't half bad. Since the Big D, Mom had been trying to work a little bit less and pay a little more attention to meals and housecleaning and other home stuff. And surprisingly, she and Mom were having a lot of fun together during the snow days.

Aimee grabbed her scarf and coat. "Come over and we'll drive to the lake in a little while."

"You didn't say what you're wearing," Madison said.

"My lemon-drop ski parka, what do you think?" Aimee said. "It's been waiting to make its ice-skating debut. And my new jeans with the embroidery up the sides. Oh, Maddie, I planned my outfit like days ago. I could never ever wait until the last minute—I would just lose my mind, you know?"

As Aimee left, Madison looked in the mirror again and smiled. She was calmer than calm now. This was going to be okay. She hung the rest of her clothes back in the closet.

But then, as she was tidying her room, Madison noticed the sealed Ivy letter. She picked it up from her dresser and read the front and back, something she'd done at least fifty times since finding it. Then she turned on her dresser lamp and held the letter up to the light. *Wasn't there any writing she could see through the envelope?* She wanted desperately to know what it said.

"Drat," Madison said to herself. She couldn't see anything except for random scribbles and their names.

Madison sat down on the bed quietly. She wanted to work out a plan to bring the letter to the lake. Ivy had a right to read the letter at the same time as Madison. That was what they had promised each other. Madison needed to find some quiet time with Ivy and pull Ivy away from her evil drones.

Was this letter something that could change Ivy from enemy back into friend? Would it make up for all the yucky things that had been said and done over the past four years? Would they share a good laugh about surviving seventh grade—and even about both liking Hart Jones?

Madison curled up onto a pillow and sighed. A part of her felt like crying, but she didn't understand why. She picked up the phone and dialed Fiona's house, but the machine picked up.

Why did she feel like crying?

Madison sat upright again, determined not to feel anything.

She would give Ivy the letter and then walk away. She would let Ivy decide who should open it. That would be that.

Madison walked back over to the full-length mirror and stared at her reflection once more. "Chill out, Maddie," she told herself. "It's only a dumb letter. It's only a dumb skating party."

Mom happened to walk into the room at that exact moment and heard Madison talking to herself. "You really shouldn't say that, honey bear."

"What?" Madison said, whirling around.

"I don't like hearing you talk that way about yourself or about anyone. You are *not* dumb," Mom said.

"Oh." Madison gulped. "I didn't know you were standing there."

"You are a beautiful young lady. And that sweater looks dreamy on you, if I may say so. Your mother has good taste, right?" Mom said.

Madison nodded. "Yeah. It's just that I get so nervous about doing things I'm not good at. And skating is one of those things. And then there's this boy . . ."

"Boy?" Mom asked. "You mean Egg?"

"What?" Madison said. "Eeew! Yuck! *No!* Someone else."

"You mean someone who's going to be at the lake, too?" Mom asked.

Madison nodded. "So I have to look right. I have to act right. I have to—"

"You have to *be yourself*, sweetie. This boy will like you just fine if you have a good time and be yourself."

"But what is being myself, Mom?" Madison sighed. "I just don't know."

Mom smiled. "Oh, Maddie, I wish I could take all your nerves away. Come here."

Mom hugged Madison. Then she helped her comb her hair so it wouldn't have so much static. The digital clock read 10:52. Madison had to hurry.

"Good luck!" Mom waved good-bye from the porch. Madison waved back and sped over to Aimee's house, trying to avoid ice slicks and slush puddles along the way. She had on her rainbow cap, green gloves, and orange parka and her new orange sweater and jeans.

Most important, the Ivy letter was neatly jammed into the inside pocket of her coat.

Roger, Aimee's oldest brother, drove the girls over to the lake. He had a bad cold and kept sneezing the whole time, so Madison and Aimee huddled in the backseat as far away from the germs as they could get. They didn't want to get sick, the way Fiona had been all week. By the time they passed through the gate marked WELCOME TO LAKE WANNALOTTA, the skating party came into view. Almost everyone else was already there. Madison could see Egg speeding around the lake, showing off his new hockey skates. Drew was following right behind him with his digital camera. Ivy and her drones were huddled by a bench. About a dozen other kids who weren't in the seventh grade were there, too.

"I haven't skated yet this winter! I am so psyched," Aimee said as she leaped out of her family's minivan. Madison wanted to stay in the backseat and go back home with Roger, but she finally did get out, skates in hand.

"Hey, Finnster!" someone yelled.

Hart.

Madison felt her cheeks blush. She wasn't prepared to say hello, so she let Hart do most of the talking. He rushed right over, also carrying his skates in his hands.

"Whatcha been doing during the snowstorm?" he asked, babbling on and on about the weather. Madison couldn't understand why he was talking so fast—or why he was talking *to her*. Out of the corner of her eye, she saw Ivy give a dirty look in her direction.

"We'd better put our skates on," Madison said. She felt warm.

"I knew you'd come," Egg said, walking over to both of them. He was walking on the ground but wearing his skates.

After five minutes, with Aimee's assistance, Madison's skates were tied up and she was ready to hit the ice. Hart was still struggling with one of his laces, which had broken.

"See you out there," Madison said, wobbling over to the ice. There was a splintered wooden deck built on one edge of the lake where people could enter and exit.

Sssssssssssst!

Chet skidded to a stop on the edge of his blades, sending up an ice spray.

"Hey, Maddie!" Chet said. "Fiona said to say hi to you and Aimee. She's almost better. Mom says you guys can come over Sunday if you want. Actually, I think we're gonna have everyone over for hot chocolate."

"Really? Great!" Madison said.

Chet spun around in a circle like some kind of professional skater.

"Where did you learn to do *that*?" Madison asked him. "You're from California."

"So? We skate there, too," Chet said, laughing. "Are you skating or what?"

Madison was about to make up some excuse, but then Egg skated by and pushed Chet. He took off to chase Egg around the ring. Across the ice, they caught up with Drew, Lance, Suresh, and some other kids from school.

"Madison?" Dan Ginsburg was standing right behind her. "I figured you'd be here. Cool."

"Hey, Dan," Madison said, smiling. "Everyone is here."

"Are Ivy and Hart going out or what?" Dan asked.

Madison's mouth dropped open. "Huh?"

"Look over there. I heard he was a good skater, so why is he letting *her* show him how to skate? How dorky is that?" Dan laughed and skated off.

Madison shoved her hands into her pockets. She felt the letter and pulled it out. Maybe I should just rip this up, she thought. But she put it back into her pocket again.

She could see that Ivy was actually grabbing Hart's hand and pulling him along the ice. *She was touching him!* Rose and Joan were following like good drones. Madison looked away.

Across the ice, Aimee was doing some kind of pirouette. Madison was amazed. Aimee was excellent at ballet, skating, and so many other things. Some cute boy was already talking to her on the ice, too.

"Maddie!" Aimee shouted, and waved. "Get out here. It's FUN!"

Madison tentatively stepped out on the ice. Her legs started to slide apart like she'd do a split, but she was able to steady herself quickly. She pushed off with her right foot but couldn't quite push off with her left. This meant that when she tried to skate, all she did was go around in circles.

Aimee came over when she saw Madison wavering on the ice. "Gotcha," Aimee said, sweeping in and putting her arm on Madison's arm.

"Aimee, I can't do this," Madison said. Her knees *and* voice were shaking.

"Yes, you can," Aimee said. She pulled Madison along by the side and then switched over to skating in front. As Aimee skated backward, she pulled Madison along with her.

"Cowabunga!" Egg screamed from the middle of

90

nowhere. He skated right toward the two girls. Aimee jumped back, but before Madison knew what had hit her, she was lying flat on her back.

"Jerk!" Aimee yelled at Egg as he zipped away, laughing hysterically. She leaned down to help Madison up off the frozen lake. "Are you okay, Maddie?"

"Yeah," Madison said. She could see that almost everyone was staring at her now, like they were waiting for her next round of ice acrobatics.

"You wanna keep skating?" Aimee asked.

They circled the ice once together. "I need to stop for a minute," Madison said. She clung to the edge of the ice, holding on to the railing, while Aimee skated off. Next to her was a girl she'd never met before, who introduced herself as Susie Quinby.

"Where do you go to school?" Madison asked.

"Actually, I go to boarding school. I'm just home on break," Susie said.

"Really?" Madison said. "So where in Far Hills do you live?"

"Well, do you know where Hart Jones lives? I'm his next-door neighbor. And he's the one who invited me here. He's wicked nice."

"*Really?*" Madison said. For a brief moment, she let go of the railing, which sent her body sliding back into the middle of the lake.

"Madison?" Susie called out.

But in a matter of seconds the damage was done.

Madison Finn felt her body swirl around the ice before landing with a hard smack.

She'd fallen.

And she couldn't get up.

Chapter 9

"Is this yours?" Susie was leaning over Madison, holding the Ivy letter.

Madison finally lifted herself up. The ice was cold on her butt. "Yes, that's mine!" she said, grabbing the letter and shoving it back into her pocket.

"What happened over here?" Egg said, skating up to investigate the fall. "One minute you're gliding over the ice, and the next minute you're—SLAM!"

"Very funny, Egg," Madison moaned, struggling to her feet.

Ivy skated over. "Ouch, that must have hurt." She snickered. Most of the other kids around Madison giggled, too.

"Hey, Finnster," Hart said as he checked in, too.

"HEY, EVERYONE!" Egg cried out from across the ice. "IT'S TIME TO PICK TEAMS!"

"Why do we need to pick teams?" Madison asked aloud.

Drew said, "Ice tag's better that way!"

Everyone skated off toward the middle of the lake to play, but Madison collapsed on a bench instead.

"What are you doing over here?" Aimee asked, joining her on the bench.

"I can't play ice tag," Madison said, making a face. "I'll just watch."

"Then I'll watch, too," Aimee said, sitting.

"GET OUT HERE, AIM! WE NEED YOU!" Egg yelled from the ice.

"Let's just start the game," Ivy complained. "If she wants to sit out, then let her."

"Hey, Finnster!" Hart shouted. He was a little unsteady on his skates, but he threw his arms into the air and glided across the ice. "It's easy! Come on!"

Madison laughed. She shot a look at Ivy. "Okay!" she said cheerily. Aimee grabbed her hand, and together they went out to the middle of the ice.

Ivy stood there frozen, arms crossed, with an angry glare on her face.

Rose skated by Madison and said, "No one is going to pick you for their team if you can't skate, Madison."

Madison was shocked. How could she say something so mean in front of everyone else? But no one else was listening. Not even Aimee.

Should she go back to the bench?

Madison glanced over at Ivy, who had wiggled herself over a little closer to Hart. She looked so pretty. Ivy wore red velvet jeans, a blue turtleneck sweater, and a denim jacket with fleece inside. She was the best-dressed skater on the lake, for sure.

The ice tag captains were Egg and Lance. Egg chose first.

"I PICK MADISON!" Egg yelled at the top of his lungs.

Ivy scoffed. But Madison smiled. Egg was such a good friend sometimes, usually when she least expected it. He came through for her when she needed support the most—like now.

"I choose Aimee," Lance said.

Aimee skated over to his side, making a sad face at Madison. They wouldn't be on the same team, but that was okay. Madison couldn't help but laugh when she realized that out of everyone—boys and girls—she and her BFF were chosen first. That meant something.

The rest of Egg's team worked out to be Chet, Dan, Rose, and Hart. They were up against Lance, Aimee, Ivy, Suresh, Joanie, and Susie. Drew was "official game photographer." He was more into his new Christmas present than skating.

The way it worked was each team chose their

"tagger," and that person sped around the ice, tagging whomever he or she could catch. The goal was to tag people on the opposite team and send them to jail over by the tree.

Madison figured she would get tagged right away, but no one came after her. She stood off to the side, pretending to be invisible while everyone else skated around each other, giggling and screaming. If she stayed under the radar, she'd stay safe. However, as soon as Ivy was It, the attention turned in her direction.

Ivy sped over in Madison's direction, and tagged her out, knocking her down on the ice.

Madison saw Drew snap a digital photo at the exact moment of contact.

Great shot.

Ivy brushed off her hands and skated away. Madison was left alone at the tree, while everyone else seemed miles away.

What she wanted to do was kick off her ice skates and run as fast as she could away from the lake, away from all these people, *away*!

But she didn't have to run. All at once Aimee skated toward her, much to the protests of her teammates.

"Maddie," Aimee whispered. "I'll keep you company."

Madison shook her head. "That's not fair, Aim, you're not out."

A moment later, Hart's neighbor Susie skated over, too. "I saw what that girl did, Madison," Susie said. "I'll get her back for you."

Aimee smiled. "We *both* will."

"But she's on your team," Madison said.

"Maybe," Susie said. "But she isn't very nice. She was totally unfriendly to me until I told her that I live next to Hart."

"WHAT ARE YOU GUYS DOING?" Egg yelled from across the ice.

Ivy yelled, too. "COME ON, AIMEE! SUSIE! GET BACK IN THE GAME!"

Susie and Aimee skated back on the ice, and headed right in Ivy's direction.

"Wait just a minute! I'm on your team," Ivy protested to them both.

"Whoops!" Aimee said as she pretended to trip, skating right into Ivy.

Susie skated at her from the other side. Just then Chet tagged Ivy to send her to jail.

"YOU'RE OUT, IVY!" Egg yelped, laughing.

Ivy looked around in all directions. She didn't know where to go. Rose pointed across the ice at the jail by Madison. But Ivy saw Hart, goofing around with Drew on the other side. She took the long way to the tree, so she could pass by Hart.

Madison watched as Ivy skated full speed right at him. He wasn't really paying attention. He didn't see her coming.

Whoooooomp!

The pair crashed to the ice. Everyone took a deep breath.

But then the laughter began—Ivy and Hart laughing. They were lying on top of each other on the ice, laughing like little kids.

Madison wanted to *cry*.

"Now, that is just disgusting," Aimee said, skating over toward Madison. "She is the grossest. And she is so obvious. I could just—"

"Forget it, Aim," Madison said, cutting her off.

Madison noticed Drew over at the crash site, snapping digital photos for the school Web site. She cringed at the thought that there would be a picture of Ivy and Hart on the Web for everyone to see, like they were a "couple" or something.

Madison had made Ivy pay temporarily, but as always, the enemy got the last laugh.

She reached into her pocket for the Ivy letter. It was wrinkled and a little wet from traveling all over the ice today.

"Poison Ivy Daly will never, ever, *ever* see this," Madison told herself. "Not after what she's done here. No way."

After an hour more of ice tag, Madison's toes were beginning to feel like little ice cubes. She sat on a bench, watching everyone else have a good time on the ice. Hart and Ivy skated together, talking and laughing. He didn't call out, "Hey, Finnster!" again during the whole time Madison was sitting on the bench. Ivy insisted on helping Hart skate, and he didn't seem to mind. Madison guessed the boys weren't patient enough with him since he was only a beginner. Or maybe Hart liked Ivy?

Aimee and Susie were practicing spins and turns together. Since Susie had been a competitive skater, she knew so many neat tricks. Aimee seemed thrilled to learn all the new moves. They waved to Madison from the center of the ice, looping their bodies around, making jump spins, and rotating like tops.

Madison was impressed, but she didn't venture out onto the ice to join them. She was content to sit on the bench and freeze. By now, Madison's green gloves had gotten so wet that she could barely feel her fingertips. And her rainbow hat was getting very scratchy around her hairline.

"Hey, everyone!" Chet yelled, skating over by the benches. "I want to invite all you guys over to my house Sunday afternoon!"

"COOL!" Egg yelled.

Lance, Suresh, Dan, and Joanie said they couldn't go.

Madison could see Ivy and Hart and Rose, still skating way out on the lake. They didn't make it back in time to hear Chet's announcement. She wondered if they could go. She hoped *not*.

"So it's like this," Chet continued. "My sister's

been way sick for like a week and she's better now, so we're having this hot chocolate party or whatever you want to call it."

"Hot chocolate *party*?" Susie said. "Delish. Is it okay if I come? I mean, I know I just met you guys."

"Sure," Aimee said.

Madison grinned. "You and Fiona will really like each other," she said.

"I think her brother is pretty cute," Susie said.

Aimee laughed out loud, but Madison looked over and noticed that Chet was smiling a little at Susie, too.

"Do you like any of these boys?" Susie asked.

Aimee laughed even louder. "I don't think so."

"Not really," Madison said, looking around for Hart. "No one here."

"So everyone come over Sunday around one," Chet repeated. "I'll send you guys an e-mail with my address and all that."

Everyone began to disperse. Kids were running around in all directions, looking for mittens, skates, and where their rides had parked. Just as Aimee's brother Roger pulled in, someone threw a snowball and it landed on Roger's windshield.

Madison saw Aimee's dog, Blossom, in the front seat. Blossom poked her big basset hound snout out through the cracked-open window.

"Wowwwwwffff!" Blossom barked.

Madison raced over to the minivan and petted

Blossom's head. "Hey, Roger," she said. "Aimee's taking off her skates. She'll be here in a sec."

"Snowball fight, eh?" Roger said, chuckling. "Someone's going to get beaned. You better get in the car."

Madison climbed in just in time to see a snowball narrowly miss Aimee's head. She stood up, indignant, and made her own snowball, whirling it toward Drew and Egg.

Within moments, a snowball war had broken out. Chet hurled snow at Aimee, who hurled snow at Lance, who hurled snow at Susie, who tried to hide behind one of the benches.

Drew got socked on the shoulder and yelled at some kid because he feared his new camera would get wet.

At the same time, Ivy, Hart, and Rose were coming off the ice. Madison couldn't believe the way Hart was following Ivy around like a puppy dog. They weren't paying much attention to the snowball fight that had gotten under way, at least not at first. Ivy was talking and tossing her red hair like she always did.

But then Chet sent a snowball flying in their direction. It narrowly missed all three of them.

"Whoa!" Hart yelped. He ducked down so he wouldn't get beaned.

Ivy, on the other hand, didn't duck fast enough.
Sploooch!

A superslick snowball landed right on the side of

her head. Her beautiful red hair turned into a wet mess.

"Oh my God!" Aimee cried from behind the bench. Susie clapped.

Ivy stood there for a moment without moving.

"Are you okay?" Hart said, trying to help her get the ice off her face and shoulder.

"What are you smiling at?" Ivy cried. "Someone intentionally threw that snowball, and you know who you are!"

Hart giggled. "Well, it is just a snowball, Ivy."

Rose giggled at that, too.

"What are *you* laughing at?" Ivy snapped at Rose. "This hurts. You're supposed to be on my side."

"It's just a little red," Rose said. "You'll be okay." *Splooooch!*

Another snowball whizzed past and landed on the ice.

"STOP THAT!" Ivy screeched.

By now Aimee noticed Roger's minivan. She said good-bye to Susie and dashed over to the car.

"Hey, Blossom!" Aimee cried, getting into the front seat. Roger backed up and headed out of the Lake Wannalotta parking lot.

"Maddie, did you see that snowball fight?" Aimee asked. "Ivy almost got hit twice!"

"You'll notice I got into the car when the snow started to fly," Madison said.

"Yeah, well, I think that is the funniest thing I

have ever seen. Chet was aiming for Hart, and he hit Ivy! Serves her right! She looked soooo mad!"

Aimee and Madison howled with laughter. Blossom joined in.

Madison was readier than ready to leave behind this long day of skating. Not only had she crashed, bottom down, on the ice, but after everything that happened, she had never shown Ivy the sealed letter. She wasn't able to find five minutes alone to share the letter with Ivy. Should she hide the letter in the attic again and try to forget she'd ever found it?

But she couldn't forget.

As they drove onward, Madison got more excited about getting home to her warm clothes, good eats, and most of all—to her own doggie.

She wanted to give Phinnie a giant pug hug before taking him out for his post-blizzard walk. She'd figure out what to do with the letter . . .

Later.

Chapter 10

"Mom!" Madison cried as she walked into the house. "Mom? I'm home from skating." She removed her hat and gloves and headed over to the kitchen for a warm drink.

"Oh, Maddie!" Mom wailed. She came running out from the kitchen, carrying the portable phone. "Oh, Maddie!"

"What?" Madison cried. In a split second all the worst-possible things that could ever happen raced through her mind.

"Oh, Maddie!" Mom kept saying the same thing over and over.

"Is it Dad? Is it Gramma?" Madison asked. "What's wrong?"

"*Phinnie!*" Mom cried again. "I took him out for a long walk, and when we came back, I must have left the door open a crack because the next thing I knew, he was gone. He's *gone*!"

Madison fell backward onto the couch. "Gone? That's not possible!"

"I drove around the neighborhood. I was just calling that nice lady Eileen over at the Far Hills Clinic in case someone reports finding a missing pug. Oh, I don't know what else to do."

"Phin is *lost*?" Madison said, still not believing what was happening.

"Not lost, exactly. Oh, I think he ran away. I'm so sorry, honey bear," Mom said. She threw her arms around Madison's shoulders.

Madison broke free and tugged on her rainbow hat again. She grabbed Phin's leash, which was hanging on a hook in the hall. "I have to find him."

"He's never, ever done this before," Mom said. "He has to be somewhere nearby."

Madison raced for the front door. "I'll go look for him. Mom, you stay here in case he comes home."

"I don't want you looking by yourself," Mom said. She looked heartbroken.

"I'll just make a loop around Blueberry Street. I know where he likes to sniff and play. Maybe he headed over to Aimee's to see Blossom?"

"I checked. But you should check again. I'll call over there and let Aimee know you're coming. Maybe she can help you search."

But Madison didn't want any help. She had to find Phinnie on her own.

First she walked their usual short route down Blueberry Street and looping back. She checked all the bushes and areas where Phin loved to sniff most.

"Phinnie!" Madison cried. *"Phinnie!"*

One of their next-door neighbors, a real estate broker named Olga, was out shoveling her driveway. Madison waved and asked if she'd seen Phin, but she hadn't. She offered to drive Madison around, but Madison wanted to walk.

Around the corner from them, Madison checked out what was happening at a small playground with a swing set and monkey bars. Sometimes Phinnie liked to run around and play near there, although they hadn't been since the summer. Three little kids were building a snowman.

"Have you seen a dog?" Madison asked.

"I don't like dogs," one little girl said.

"Oh." Madison didn't know what to say to that. The little kids went back to building their snowman.

She turned onto Ridge Road, where Fiona and Chet lived. There were a bunch of old Victorian homes on this block with big yards and other dogs. She saw Charlie, a Dalmatian, playing in the snow. His owner was on the porch.

"Hello?" Madison called out. "Have you seen my little dog?"

"You're the one with the pug, right?" the man

asked. Madison nodded, and the man said, "Nope. Sorry."

Charlie came over to Madison, wagging his tail. Her heart sank. Was Phin lost for good?

But she kept walking.

At the end of Ridge Road was a small pond. Sometimes Phin would get curious about frogs and the water. But the pond was a sheet of ice, and Madison couldn't see him anywhere in the area.

"Phinnie?" she yelled out. She could feel her voice wavering. Madison was getting sad and frustrated. Phin had never run away before. Why did he pick today to run?

"Madison?" a voice cried from behind her.

It was Rose Thorn. Madison's stomach flip-flopped. The last person she needed to see right now was one of Ivy's drones.

"Hi, Rose," Madison said. She realized that she'd been standing in Rose's backyard.

"What are you doing?" Rose asked.

"I lost my dog," Madison wailed. "My pug, Phinnie."

"Bummer," Rose said. "Where did you lose him?"

"If I knew that . . ." Madison started to say.

"Does he run away a lot?" Rose asked. "My cat runs away, but she always comes back."

"Cats and dogs are different."

"Well, where do you think he ran?" Rose asked.

"I don't know. I thought the park. Then I checked

the pond. And the streets where I usually walk him."
Madison sighed. "I don't know. And he doesn't like
the cold. His little paws get all frozen, so he can't
walk right."

"Do you want help looking for him?" Rose asked.

Madison looked at her with disbelief. "Huh?"

"Let me help you look. If we split up, we can do
it faster," Rose said.

Madison wondered why she would have turned
down help from one of her biggest supporters,
Mom, and now take help from one of her biggest
enemies, Rose. But she did.

"Okay," Madison said. "If you really want to
help."

Rose went into her house for her hat and gloves,
and they continued around the neighborhood
together.

Ten minutes later, the pair had looked on four
other blocks with no luck.

"Maybe I should just check back at my house,"
Madison said. Then she saw Mom's car pulling up
beside them on the street.

"I couldn't just sit there at home," Mom said. She
turned to Rose and said, "I'm Madison's mom. Are
you a friend of Maddie's?"

Rose shrugged. "We're in school together. We
can't find your dog anywhere. And I have to get
home now."

"Thanks, Rose," Madison said. "I mean it."

"I hope you find Phin," Rose said.

"Thanks," Madison said, and waved good-bye.

"Why haven't you ever mentioned Rose before?" Mom asked as Madison climbed into the front seat of the car. "She seems nice."

"Not really," Madison said abruptly. She covered her face with her hands. "Mom, I don't know what I'll do if Phinnie is gone. I'll be sad forever."

They stopped by Aimee's house one more time. Phin wasn't there.

"How long has he been missing now?" Mrs. Gillespie asked.

Madison frowned. "An hour. And it's getting dark."

"Well, I'll get the boys out to help you look," Mrs. Gillespie said. She called for Roger and Billy and asked them to drive around the other sides of the neighborhood while Madison and her mom checked door-to-door.

They must have rung a dozen different doorbells, but no one remembered seeing a little pug.

Phinnie *was* lost.

"Thanks, boys," Mom said to Roger and Billy when she sent them home a while later. She tried to console Madison with a hug, but Madison pulled away.

"We can put up posters around the neighborhood. And I'll try calling Eileen again."

As they pulled into the driveway, Madison began

to cry. She couldn't imagine spending a night without her beloved Phin. They got out of the car and headed for the porch.

"Rowrorooooo!"

"Mom?" Madison's eyes widened. "Did you hear that?"

Mom clapped, and they both started running toward the front door. Phin was there, with his curlicue tail wagging as fast as his little bottom could shake.

"Phinnie!" Madison screeched. She threw her arms around him and buried her teary face in his coarse fur. "He came home!"

"Thank goodness," Mom said.

Madison lifted Phin up and carried him inside while Mom hurried to call the Gillespies and everyone else who had helped them look for Phin around the neighborhood.

"Nice dog breath, Phin!" Madison said, pulling her head away from his nonstop kisses. They headed upstairs, where Madison could towel him off (he'd been out in the cold for so long!). Together they curled up on her comforter for a reunion snooze.

Phin just wheezed and wheezed, happy to be warm—and happier than happy to be home.

That night, Mom made soup and sandwiches for dinner. Madison wasn't all that hungry from the day's excitement, but she joined Mom at the table, anyway.

"While you and the runaway dog were napping, your father called," Mom said with a smile.

"What did Dad want?" Madison asked.

"He's trying to get a flight home Monday or Tuesday. The airport in Denver is still messed up. The storms are in Colorado and out west now. It's a travel nightmare, Dad said."

Madison missed Dad. He'd been gone for almost a week now.

"So he's coming over when he gets back?" Madison asked.

"Yes, honey bear. He'll be here. He promised."

Madison yawned. "I'm so tired, Mom," she said. "I think I'm going to go upstairs and go to bed for real."

"Well, it's been some day, Maddie. I don't blame you. And I'm sure Phinnie is tired, too."

They kissed good night, and Madison headed back up to her room.

She went to crawl into bed but stopped herself on the way. Her laptop was sitting open on her desk but she hadn't checked her e-mail since the power outage the night before.

In the half darkness of her bedroom, she logged on to bigfishbowl.com.

Phin curled up at her feet.

From: MadFinn
To: Bigwheels
Subject: Hello
Date: Thurs 18 Jan 7:23 PM

How are you???? I just checked the
site to see if I could IM you, but
you aren't online. Today was without
a doubt the strangest EVER. I went
skating, but that wasn't everything.
So much happened! Phin ran away,
Ivy got hit with a snowball, and
way more than that. I'll tell you
all about it the next time we
Insta-Message. I'm too tired to
repeat it all right now. I'm going
to bed and it isn't even eight
o'clock at night!

Please write back sooner than soon.
I miss you, Bigwheels!

Yours till the snow drifts,

MadFinn

p.s. I'm putting another picture of
Phinnie on here. Mom took this
during the blizzard. Yikes! Snow
dog!
Attachment: PHINSTORM.jpg

Madison yawned again. Her eyes felt droopy. But she could see that she had some e-mail, and she was too curious not to look.

```
From: Wetwins
To: The Skates
Subject: Cocoa Party SUNDAY
Date: Thurs 18 Jan 7:01 PM
```

Hello everybody, the party is ON!!!!!!!!!!! This is where Chet and Fiona live: 23 Ridge Road (near intersection of Walker Avenue). Be there at one o'clock. We are making food and hot chocolate, and we'll be doing something fun like playing videos or games. SO be there or be a loser!!!! LOL L8R 4 U!

Madison scanned the e-mail to see if she could figure out the list of people who had been invited. She remembered that Ivy hadn't been standing around when Chet told everyone else about the party. Maybe that meant Ivy wouldn't be asked? Maybe she wouldn't show up?

Madison hoped as hard as she possibly could that Ivy was left off the list. She hoped so hard, she crossed her fingers, toes, *and* eyes.

But then she saw a second e-mail in her box with the same subject line. Unfortunately it was from Ivy, who'd hit REPLY ALL when she got Chet's message. This meant she *had* been invited.

```
From: Flowr99
To: Wetwins
Cc: The Skates
Subject: Re: Cocoa Party SUNDAY
Date: Thurs 18 Jan 7:31 PM
```

```
Fab! I will TOTALLY see you there,
Chet. Thank you again for inviting
me. TTFN.
:>) Ivy
```

Why was Madison so haunted this week by letters from Ivy? Some she could open . . . and some she couldn't open, but the letters followed her *everywhere*.

Madison wanted to screech.

She opened up a new file instead.

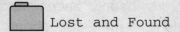 Lost and Found

```
    I thought the real snow that falls from
the sky was bad enough, but boy, was I ever
WRONG! There are worse storms in my life
like I-V-Y. How come she acts so superior
to everyone else? And how come she keeps
showing up wherever I am? I really doubt if
```

Fiona would have invited the enemy over! Chet is a chucklehead.

Skating was a disaster. I felt invisible. And Hart pretended to be all nice, but I think he sees me more like a friend and nothing else. At least I hope he sees me like a friend! Aimee whispered to me today that he is always looking at me and asked if I liked him. I could have swallowed my gum! No way, I said. NO ONE LIKES HART except for Poison Ivy. I hate lying to Aimee, but she can't know. I would die of embarrassment if everyone knew that I liked the same person as Poison Ivy.

Just when I think I'm done finding out everything I can about Ivy, she somehow makes my life miserable AGAIN. Like now I STILL have this sealed letter that I found. I keep trying to blow it off—and it keeps coming back to bug me!!! The new plan is that I will show it to her at the party and that will be the end of it. She thinks she knows everything, but I will show her a few things. HA!

Rude Awakening: No one likes a snow-it-all.

Ivy's the real blizzard around here. Just when I think she's gone, she slams me harder than before.

But she better watch out.

This weekend, I'm ready to slam back.

Chapter 11

"You look soooooo good!" Aimee squealed as she and Madison walked into the Waterses' house together.

It was a half hour before Sunday's party's official "start time." They wanted to arrive early and hang out with Fiona alone for a while.

"I missed you guys so much!" Fiona cooed. She coughed a little. "You shouldn't get too close, though. Just in case I'm still contagious or something."

"I missed you, too, Fiona!" Madison leaned in for a squeeze. "And I don't care if I catch your flu. Being sick would be better than everything that's been happening to me."

"I heard that Phin ran away," Fiona said. "But he's okay now, right?"

"Yeah," Madison said. "He had me so scared."

They walked into the kitchen, where Mr. and Mrs. Waters were both putting food out on trays. They had prepared a fondue pot with melted chocolate, marshmallow crispy treats, and other fun munchies.

"Have some!" Mrs. Waters handed Aimee a brownie, but she refused.

"I'm on a diet," she said.

Madison rolled her eyes and took the brownie. "I'll try it," she said, smiling.

"You know there are like a thousand calories in just one brownie," Aimee said. Madison ate it, anyway.

In the living room, a VCR was set up with movies so kids could watch TV if they wanted. In the down-stairs family room, another area was set up so every-one could hang out and listen to music.

"This is a real party," Aimee said, impressed. "I thought we'd just be hanging out talking and eating and drinking cocoa. This is serious, Fiona."

"Well, my parents like to overdo everything," Fiona admitted. "They always want us to have a good time."

Madison and Aimee giggled.

Madison loved being at Fiona's house before the party started . . . before Ivy Daly came.

She felt around inside her jacket just to make sure the letter was still there. As soon as she got rid of the letter, she'd lose all memories of her enemy.

Dingdong.

Egg and Drew arrived and went into the living room with Chet. They hooked up the PlayStation and started to play without saying hello to Mr. and Mrs. Waters or the girls.

Fiona grabbed a potato chip and took a seat in the dining room. She wanted to be filled in on all the gossip from ice skating.

Who skated with whom? What happened on the ice?

Most important, she wanted to know . . . what was *Egg* doing the whole time? Her major crush on Egg didn't go away even when she hadn't seen him in days.

Dingdong. Dingdong.

Ivy and Hart, by coincidence, arrived at the exact same time.

Madison hated coincidences. It was the superstitious side of her acting up. She figured that this coincidence meant Ivy would be sitting next to Hart the whole time they were at Fiona's (when not surrounded by her drones, of course).

Madison kept a hawk's eye on her enemy during the start of the party. She had to find the right time to bring out the letter.

But when?

She almost followed Ivy into the bathroom once, until Ivy shot her a look.

"I think I was here first," Ivy said, shutting the door. "You'll have to wait."

There was another moment in the middle of eating when Madison found herself in the kitchen alone with Ivy. But all she could do was stare. She had a total speech block.

"Do you have a problem?" Ivy asked.

Madison took a mouthful of chips. "No," she said, chewing. "I was just zoning out. Sorry."

"Whatever," Ivy grunted.

As Ivy walked away, Madison fingered the letter inside her pocket. Why couldn't she let go? Why couldn't she just tell her the truth? The longer Madison waited to share the sealed letter . . . the bigger deal it became.

After everyone had eaten plates of food from the kitchen, Chet gathered the group in the family room with Twister. But no one really felt like playing a game where you had to bend and crouch.

"We just ate," Dan said. "My stomach is way too full."

He burped for emphasis.

"How gross," Aimee said.

He burped again.

"I know! Let's play truth or dare instead," Ivy suggested.

Fiona started to say, "I don't really want to—"

But Egg interrupted. "Totally!" he said. "Excellent idea. Truth or dare."

The group sat on the floor in a circle. Ivy sat next

to Hart, just as Madison had predicted. Everyone else sat mostly boy-girl, boy-girl.

"We should actually play spin the bottle truth or dare," Ivy said, amending her original suggestion.

"What's *that*?" Madison asked.

Ivy demonstrated.

"You spin the bottle and it lands on someone like this." She grabbed a soda bottle from the table and spun it around on the floor. "So in this case it landed on Rose. Now, I ask Rose, 'Truth or dare?' "

"Dare!" Rose blurted.

"Okay." Ivy laughed. "So now I think up a really, really good dare. Like, spin the bottle again and you have to kiss the person it lands on."

"Kiss?" Aimee exclaimed.

"I don't want to play this game, Ivy," Fiona said.

"Oh, don't be a baby," Chet said to his sister. "It'll be really fun."

Aimee leaned over to Fiona. "Maybe it won't be terrible. Let's try."

"Okay, so who's going to start?" Ivy asked. She handed the bottle to her left to Drew. He smiled as he took it.

Drew spun. It pointed back to himself, and everyone in the room laughed.

He spun again, and it landed on Hart's friend Susie.

"So what do I do?" Drew asked.

"Truth or dare?" Ivy reminded him.

He asked Susie which she wanted.

"Truth," Susie said, without missing a beat. "Absolutely."

"Okay." Drew thought for a minute. "Have you ever been to a foreign country?"

"Wait, wait!" Ivy blurted. "What kind of a question is *that*?"

"You didn't say there was a special kind of question I was supposed to ask," Drew said.

"Well, everyone knows that you're supposed to ask better ones than that," Ivy said. "No one cares if she went to a foreign country."

"I do," Madison said.

"I have a better question!" Egg said. He whispered it to Drew.

"Okay." Drew changed his question. "What's the most embarrassing thing that has ever happened to you?"

Susie smiled. She thought for a moment.

Hart cracked up. "I know that one, Susie. Don't lie!"

"Hart, be quiet!" Susie said. "Let me see. . . ."

Ivy made a face. "What are you talking about, Hart?"

"Let Susie answer," Madison said to Ivy. Of course she was curiouser than curious about what Susie and Hart had meant by that comment, too.

"Well, I guess you're right, Hart," Susie said, looking over at Hart again. "That *was* the most embarrassing thing ever. Well, this summer . . . Hart saw me naked."

"WHAT?" Ivy and Madison screamed at the same time.

Ivy covered her mouth. "Get out!"

Fiona giggled.

"You're joking!" Rose blurted.

And the rest of the boys started to laugh, especially Drew. He even started to snort.

"I only saw for a second," Hart corrected her. "And I didn't even know what had happened. But Susie was so embarrassed. She kept apologizing every time she saw me. It was embarrassing for both of us."

Madison couldn't understand how something like that could have happened between Hart and Susie. How could they even look at each other?

Ivy obviously couldn't believe it, either. She had a look on her face like she'd bitten into a lemon.

"Who's next?" Drew said, passing the bottle over to Susie.

Susie spun, and it landed on Chet, which made her laugh. Madison remembered that she'd admitted during skating that she thought Chet was cute.

"DARE!" Chet said. "I am not revealing any truth to you guys. No way."

"Okay, Chet," Susie said. "Then spin the bottle and whoever it points to . . . you have to carry them around the room."

"What?" Egg shouted. "That is so stupid."

"As long as you don't have to carry me," Dan said. Except for a series of gross-out burps, he hadn't spoken much until now. Everyone laughed at the comment, though, since he was the heaviest kid in the room.

Chet spun the bottle. It landed on his sister.

"NO problem, man," Chet said. He lifted Fiona into a piggyback position and circled the family room, throwing her on the sofa at the end of it.

"Thanks a LOT," Fiona said as she crawled back down to the floor.

"Hey," Susie said, smiling. "I was going to tell him he had to lick someone's arm. Be glad I picked the piggyback thing instead."

Chet spun the bottle again and asked Ivy if she wanted truth or dare.

She thought for a moment and then said, "Truth."

Everyone wanted to tell Chet what question to ask, but he didn't want to hear anyone else. He already had a question in mind.

Madison couldn't believe Ivy had chosen truth. But Madison also suspected that Ivy would probably lie about whatever she was asked.

"Which teacher do you have the biggest crush on and why?" Chet asked.

Everyone groaned.

"Why didn't he ask her which person in the room

she had a crush on?" Fiona whispered. "My brother is a dork."

"SHHHHHH!" Chet said. "So what's your answer, Ivy?"

"Well, I would have to say . . . Mr. Danehy," Ivy said. "Because science is my favorite subject."

"What a lie," Madison said out loud.

"Excuse me?" Ivy said. "That is not a lie. Are you calling me a liar?"

"I'm your science partner, and it is SO a lie. And a big, fat, slimy one at that."

"Well, I answered the question, so I get to spin," Ivy said, ignoring Madison and twisting the bottle around on the floor.

Madison's heart sank when she saw where the bottle landed. On her.

"Well, Madison!" Ivy said with glee. "Okay, so do you want truth or dare?"

Madison looked over at Aimee for some kind of life preserver, but Aimee was distracted. Fiona was gazing off into space somewhere, too.

"I'll pick truth," she said at last. "Truth."

"Okay, then," Ivy said. She rubbed her hands together like some mad scientist. "Tell the group what person at school you have the biggest crush on and why."

The whole room tilted. Madison felt her hands get sweaty, too.

She had to lie.

"Um . . . well, no one, really . . ." Madison stammered.

"That is SO not true, Madison," Ivy said. "And you know it."

Madison blinked. "How would you know?" she asked.

Ivy smirked. "Because I do. You have to tell the truth, Madison. Spill it."

The whole circle of friends got silent. Everyone's eyes were on Madison. Even Hart was staring at her.

"We're waiting . . ." Ivy said.

Madison grabbed her knees and rocked back and forth a little.

"Okay, Ivy." Madison took a deep breath. "You got me. I will admit my crush to everyone in this room. I have a crush on Egg Diaz."

"WHAT?" Egg said. "You are the world's worst liar!"

"No lie, Egg," Madison said. "So there. Can I spin the bottle now?"

Ivy sat backward on her hands. "I guess." She looked confused.

Egg was shaking his head. "No way, man!"

Drew started snorting again.

Fiona nudged Madison before she spun the bottle. "Did you mean that, Maddie, about having a crush on Egg?"

Madison shook her head. "No way."

Fiona breathed a sigh of relief. "I thought so, but . . . you were so convincing."

"Are you going to spin the bottle or what?" Rose asked.

The bottle whirred around so fast that it moved halfway across the floor inside their circle.

"Hart!" Drew shouted.

"Truth or dare, Hart?" Aimee asked.

Madison looked him squarely in the eye. "Well?"

He looked right back at Madison and said, "Truth. Let me have it."

Madison grinned. "Okay."

Right then and there, she decided to ask him a real question. She knew Hart wouldn't lie no matter what. So she took a chance.

"Have you ever liked anyone in this room?" Madison asked. "And I mean 'like' like, not 'good friend' like. You know?"

"I know what you mean," Hart said.

He sat back and looked around the room.

Everyone waited for his answer.

Chapter 12

"The truth is, I do like someone in this room," Hart said. He didn't look at anyone in particular.

Fiona giggled.

"You do?" Madison asked again. "So the answer is 'yes'?"

"Yeah," he said.

"Oh, man!" Egg said. "Who is it? Who is it? Come on!"

"That wasn't part of the question," Hart said. "I don't have to answer with a name unless it's part of the question, right?"

Madison nodded. And of course, she'd purposefully left the name part out. She felt her heart beating, like she'd swallowed something huge.

He liked her?

Maybe.

"Your turn to spin, Hart!" Ivy said. He smiled at her and picked up the bottle. This time it landed on Egg.

He picked dare.

"Okay, then," Hart said, daring him. "I like Ivy's suggestion. Spin the bottle and then you have to kiss the person it lands on."

"Get out of here!" Egg shrieked. "What if it lands on YOU, bozo?"

"Pucker up!" Drew said.

Egg looked nervous. He spun the bottle.

"Aaaaaaaaaaaaah!" Fiona screamed. It landed on her.

"No way, man, I am NOT kissing her. She's sick," Egg said. "I'll catch some nasty germs."

"I'm all better, actually," Fiona said. "You won't get sick."

"Yeah, well, I won't risk it."

"You can't blow this off, Egg. It's the game. Everyone else played fair," Dan said. "Kiss her."

"Kiss her! Kiss her! Kiss her!" everyone started to chant.

Aimee stood up. "Hold it!" she said. "Everyone needs to stop. Chet and Fiona's mom and dad will hear us."

"You didn't say where I have to kiss her," Egg said.

Fiona blushed.

Egg leaned across the circle and kissed Fiona's bent knee.

"There!" he said, proud of himself.

"We need to get more specific about the questions in this game," Ivy said. "Like if we ask people who they like, we ask for names. And real kisses are required."

"That *was* a real kiss, Ivy," Egg argued. "Why do you have to see everyone get embarrassed?"

Ivy just shrugged. "I don't," she said. "I just—I don't."

She cut herself off. The room was silent.

"Fiona!" a voice called from outside the family room. It was Mrs. Waters. "Do you or your friends want any more snacks?" she yelled through the doorway.

The boys all jumped up for more food, but the girls stayed put.

"I think this game is history," Aimee said.

"Sure looks that way," said Susie. "I think I'm going home. I have to head back to boarding school tomorrow."

"No! Don't leave!" Fiona said. "Please?"

But everyone started to gather their stuff.

"Plus you have a math test tomorrow," Aimee reminded Madison.

"Oh, wow! The snowstorm made me forget that completely," Madison said.

"And I have ballet practice in the morning," Aimee added.

Everyone got Susie's phone number, e-mail, and

address at school so they could keep in touch. In one day she'd become a good friend.

"Let me know what happens with Hart," she whispered to Madison on her way out. No one else heard.

"Huh?" Madison said. "What are you talking about?"

"He totally likes you," Susie said. "Does anyone know you like him?"

Madison stood there like a mannequin.

"Keep in touch," she said. "I'll call if I'm home from school. And we'll have to hang over the summer."

She leaned in and gave Madison a small hug. But Madison was still too stunned by Susie's comments to move.

"Bye," Madison said, managing a one-word response.

"Bye!" Susie chirped back.

Everyone helped Chet and Fiona's parents clean up the mess around the house. Most of the food had been eaten, but no one had watched any videos. Everyone said their good-byes and bundled up to face the cold outside.

"Wanna walk home?" Madison asked Aimee. She needed some fresh air.

Aimee nodded and called her brothers to tell them she didn't need a ride home. It took them a little longer than usual to make it over to Blueberry

Street with all the black slush and puddles around the neighborhood, but the pair of BFFs made it.

"When Fiona got picked by Egg, I thought I would DIE," Aimee said. "And by the way, what was all that stuff you said about having a crush on him? Are you nuts?"

"He knows it's not true," Madison said.

"Maybe, maybe not," Aimee said. "I heard him ask Drew if you were serious."

Madison smiled. "Now, that's funny. Aimee, he knows the truth. He's one of my oldest friends."

"Yeah, but sometimes friends can change," Aimee said.

Madison stopped. They were standing in front of Aimee's place. They embraced, and Madison walked on.

"See you at school tomorrow!" Aimee called after her.

Madison nodded. She thought about Aimee's last words.

Sometimes friends can change.

Inside her pocket, the Ivy letter was now permanently warped, torn, and smudged. Madison took it out.

She ripped open the seal and read it.
Finally.

Do Not Open Till 7th Grade
Top Secret FOEO (For Our Eyes Only)

We Madison Francesca Finn and Ivy Elizabeth Daly do swear that we will be bestest friends until seventh grade and after that, too.

1. We will go to Far Hills Junior High like Janet, and we will be the coolest friends in the whole school.
2. We will always share everything and borrow each other's clothes.
3. We will get discovered by a famous TV agent and become TV stars in seventh grade. But no matter how famous we get, we will always be friends.
4. We will get married someday and have kids at the same time so they can grow up and go to school together like us.
5. We will have a farm out in the country with all kinds of animals.
6. We will travel around the world on our own plane and go swimming in all the oceans.
7. We will never be mad at each other.

After reading the letter, Madison raced home. Even though they'd been enemies now for a few years, Madison suddenly felt a blank space inside where her friendship with Ivy had been. They had all those plans together, and the only thing that had come true was their being at the same junior high school together. She knew they'd had a falling-out, but how did it get so ugly? What had *really* happened?

When Madison came inside, Mom was in her office, working on the Brazil documentary.

"Hey, Maddie!" Mom called out. "Remember those tree frogs we saw in Brazil? You have to come see the footage. It's amazing!"

Madison slunk into Mom's work space and collapsed on the floor.

"How was your party?" she asked. "You look glum."

"Huh?" Madison grunted.

"How was the party at Chet and Fiona's?"

Madison rubbed her eyes. "Okay, I guess."

Mom turned off the frog video and turned on the overhead light.

"Are you crying?" Mom asked Madison gently.

"No." Madison sniffled, wiping her nose with a tissue. "Why do you say that? I am not crying."

"What happened, honey bear?" Mom asked.

"Nothing. Everything. Oh, it's just that I think I've lost my mind, Mom. If you find it, will you let me know?"

Mom laughed. "Sure thing. You want to talk?"

"Not really," she said.

Mom nodded. "Well, I'm here when you need me."

Madison decided she would go online to surf the Internet for a pre-algebra homework helper program instead of obsessing anymore about Ivy. Thoughts of a now imminent math test were giving Madison huge tummy flip-flops. She had to get studying—fast. There were no more snowstorms to save her from the test.

The bigfishbowl.com search engine gave Madison a few different sites where she could practice her equations, multiplication of fractions, and exponents. They had a helpful hints section with special ways to remember rules and the order of things. Madison was looking for fast and easy tricks since she had so much to learn and so little time to learn it!

She learned an acronym to help her solve algebraic equations: PEMDAS (Please Eat My Delicious Apples Soon).

Instantly the whole process seemed to make sense. The letter *P* was for "parentheses," *E* was for "exponents," *M* was for "multiplication," *D* was for "division," *A* was for "addition," and *S* was for "subtraction." When she followed this order to finish her simple-variable equations, Madison felt more confident about the order of operations. Not only could she take this test, but she could ace it! Madison wondered why this part of math hadn't seemed clear before now.

What was different *now*?

After studying for a half hour, Madison opened up her files.

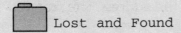 Lost and Found

Rude Awakening: I know why math is hard for me. Sometimes things just don't add up.

Why can't people stay the same? Ivy used to be so sweet. Hart used to be annoying. Life was easier a couple of years ago, before they switched places. Now Hart's the nice one, and Ivy is evil. Seventh grade has been one gigantic algebra problem, and my head is spinning.

When school at Far Hills started, they talked about how this year would be like a transition year and we'd all feel out of place and out of sorts but that would end. It would END. Well, guess what? Endings are a joke. Nothing ever **really** ends.

Like this letter thing. Now that I've read the pact I made with Ivy, I can't just throw it out. It's like a part of me. I can even remember that we signed our names with fruit-scented markers.

She closed the file and went into her e-mailbox.

FROM	SUBJECT
JeffFinn	Fw: This is SNOW funny
TRAVELUSA	Special Onetime-Only Offer
Flowr99	Science

The note from Dad turned out to be blank.

TRAVELUSA was spam.

And Flowr99 seemed familiar at first, but Madison couldn't place the address. She scanned the e-mail.

```
From: Flowr99
To: MadFinn
Subject: Science Lab Notes
Date: Sun 21 Jan 5:11 PM
```

I got your e-mail from Egg hope you don't mind. It's Sunday and I can't find any of my notes since before vacation and I need your science notes tomorrow. Bring your notebooks to class. C U L8R

Ivy hadn't signed it, but Madison knew the person who had written this.

Or at least she *used* to.

Chapter 13

Mrs. Wing was all smiles in Monday morning's computer class.

"This is a fabulous shot, Drew!" she said, looking at the computer screen in his station. Drew was downloading his digital photos from the snowstorm onto the school Web site.

"Oh no, you didn't put that one up there," Madison said when she saw the photo of her and Ivy struggling just before Madison had been "ice tagged" out. "I look so weird. Ick."

"No, you don't look weird at all, Maddie," Mrs. Wing said. "You look like you're having fun with your friends."

"Isn't that Ivy Daly?" another kid asked. "Since when are you friends with her?"

Madison dropped her head. "Since never, okay?

We were on opposite teams. Look, Drew, please take that photo off."

"But you look nice," Egg said, in his best trying-to-impress-the-teacher voice. Egg had an itsy-bitsy crush on Mrs. Wing, and when he was trying for her attention, he would often exaggerate. "Really, really nice."

"Well put, Walter," Mrs. Wing said, taking the bait.

He just grinned and crossed his arms smugly. "I know," he said.

Madison groaned.

After almost a whole week out of school, Madison and all the other students had loads of work to catch up on. It was amazing how much work seventh graders had to do. The snow days had been like frozen time—literally. But that time was long over.

Now Madison was thrust full speed ahead into schoolwork, after-school commitments, the school Web site, interschool social situations, and even gym class (which she was dreading more now than ever before).

"What about this picture?" Drew asked Madison. She looked at it close-up because she couldn't tell at first who was even shown. It was a close-up of two people who were standing on the ice, just milling around.

On the left side was Aimee and their newest

friend, Susie, and then Madison in her rainbow cap, a boy behind Madison, and Egg, hamming it up for the camera. Madison looked a little closer and could see that the unidentified boy was actually *Hart*, and he had his hand on Madison's shoulder.

Wait just a minute! Madison thought. I don't remember Hart Jones putting his hand on my shoulder or anywhere else.

She felt giddy inside.

"Skip to the next picture," Egg said, reaching for the computer mouse.

"No, I wanna see this one!" Madison said. "Can I get a copy of this one, Drew?"

Drew nodded and then scrolled through the rest of the pictures.

There was a great shot of Aimee, Rose, and Ivy. (Madison hated it, though.)

Another photo showed Chet doing a glide on only one skate. He looked like a professional. That was selected by Mrs. Wing to appear on the site.

"What did you do during the snowstorm, Mrs. Wing?" Madison asked her.

The teacher shrugged. "Not a lot. I went to help my husband over at the clinic. Have you been around there recently? They've got a bunch of brand-new cages."

"That's nice," Madison said sweetly. She missed all the animals.

Computer class zoomed by. Mrs. Wing helped

everyone in class work on their graphing skills in anticipation of the big math test. Madison was feeling more and more confident about the test—especially when she repeated her newest "simple-variable equations" mantra.

Please Eat My Delicious Apples Soon.

Please Eat My Delicious Apples Soon.

Upon entering math class, Madison sat in the front row and dumped her bag onto the floor. Taking a deep breath, she rolled up her sleeves, poised her sharpened pencil, and prepared for the worst.

But she knew the first answer right away.

And she knew the second answer, too.

In no time, Madison was whizzing onward through equations, graphs, and other algebraic mazes. She finished the dreaded math test ten minutes *early*, feeling more confident about her math skills than ever before.

On the way to lunch, Madison was in such a good mood that she stopped in to visit with Mr. Montefiore, the music teacher who led the school band. Her snow day discovery of the old flute in the attic inspired her to talk to Mr. Montefiore about taking up the instrument again.

The attic exploration had not only helped Madison to rediscover truths about friends and parents. It also helped her to find out stuff she'd forgotten about herself.

She was a good flute player. And—like it or not—she had a lot in common with her mom.

Mr. Montefiore was surprised by Madison's visit. He hadn't thought she liked to perform. But when she pulled the old flute out of her bag and played a few notes, *he* changed his tune.

"We'll get you up to speed with your band mates in no time," he reassured her. "I am very excited about this."

Madison played a little more and then put her flute back into her bag.

As she shoved it in, she saw the Ivy letter was there in the front pocket. Madison hoped that her resolve wouldn't fail.

Poison Ivy Daly would see that note today.

Everyone was still buzzing about the snow days during lunch period. Once lunch was over, however, the buzz had died down. It almost always seemed true that on the day after a school break, everyone's brains got tired more quickly. By the time science class rolled around, Mr. Danehy was dealing with a bunch of space cases.

"Did you bring the notes?" Ivy asked as soon as Madison walked into the classroom door. Madison pretended like she hadn't heard the question.

"I asked you if you brought the notes, Maddie?" Ivy asked again, a little more firmly.

"Notes?" Madison played dumb.

"I sent you an e-mail. Didn't you get it?"

"Huh?" Madison was making Ivy frustrated, but she enjoyed it.

Ivy wrinkled her eyebrows and glared at Madison. "Maddie, I have asked you the same question like seven times. Do you have the stupid science notes or what?"

"Oh!" Madison said at last. "No, I don't." She smiled.

Ivy frowned. "Aren't we supposed to be partners?" she asked.

"Yeah, so?" Madison replied.

"Well, partners help each other out. So if we have this pop quiz, then I can look on with you because you're my partner, right?"

"Pop quiz?" Madison's voice dropped. "When?"

"Where have you been?" Ivy chided. "Mr. Danehy said last week . . ."

Madison turned to face the blackboard. She hadn't even cracked her textbook open in days. Everything in the classroom slowed down. Madison started noticing that half the kids had their books out to study.

Hart came into the room just as the final bell rang. "Hey, Finnster! Ready for the quiz?"

Ivy crossed her legs with a huff. "Great, now we can both fail."

Mr. Danehy entered a moment later, but he

wasn't carrying any copies of a test. Madison closed her eyes and said a private thank-you.

"Lucky thing." Ivy snorted.

"Now, class." Mr. Danehy grabbed his pointer and directed it skyward. "There are many things in this class I'd like to point out to you." He aimed the pointer at the students. "For example, you."

Chet raised his hand. "Uh, Mr. D., are we having a pop quiz or—"

"Shhhhhhhhhhhhh!" the front row shushed him.

Mr. Danehy shook his head. "Nope. I want to talk to you about an opportunity instead. I have an opportunity for you kids to improve your grades and make an impact on your community."

"Oh no, not another community service pitch." Ivy groaned.

Madison turned to look at Hart.

When she turned, he was looking right back at her. She saw him lean into his notebook and scribble something on a sheet of paper.

Mr. Danehy kept talking. "Now, as you may know, the Far Hills Annual Science Fair is coming up soon. And I'm eager to have all of you kids involved. Please give me a show of hands. Who's interested?"

One kid in the front row raised her hand.

"Tsk! Tsk!" Mr. Danehy moaned.

Madison was listening, only at some point everything Mr. Danehy said turned into gibberish.

Madison just stared at Hart. She blinked a few

times, waiting to see what he was doing. All at once, he raised his hand, stood up, and started to walk toward Mr. Danehy's desk.

On the way there, he dropped a note onto Madison's counter.

Ivy's eyes were on the note like glue the moment it left Hart's hand.

Madison thwacked her palm over the torn piece of paper and pretended like nothing had happened.

"I saw that," Ivy whispered.

"Huh?" Madison played dumber than dumb.

"I saw." Ivy poked her nose over into Madison's airspace. "Hart dropped something right there. What was it?"

"Excuse me?" Madison asked. "I don't think that's any of your business."

"Yeah, well, I do," Ivy said.

Madison kept her palm firmly planted on the note. She wasn't going to risk Ivy seeing this—whatever it was.

Meanwhile Mr. Danehy was oblivious. He was still droning on about the science fair. Hart interrupted him to ask to go to the bathroom.

How can I read the note without Ivy seeing me? Madison thought. She looked around the room and then back over at Ivy.

Ivy hadn't taken *her* eyes off the hidden note.

"You're not supposed to pass notes in class, you know," Ivy whispered. "I can turn you in."

144

Madison laughed. "Go ahead."

Ivy raised her hand, and Madison panicked. She reached out for Ivy's arm. They ended up in a mini-tussle over the note.

"GIRLS!" Mr. Danehy yelled. "What on earth is going on back there?"

Neither Ivy nor Madison said a word.

"Madison started it," Rose spoke up from the other side of where they were sitting. "I saw her."

Ivy got a big grin on her face.

Stupid drones.

"Excuse me, Mr. Danehy," Madison said. "But I believe that Ivy Daly was passing notes, and I wouldn't pass it along for her, so she got a little—"

"You are such a liar!" Ivy huffed.

Taptaptaptaptap.

Mr. Danehy hit his desk with a ruler. "That is QUITE enough, girls," he said. "I want to see both of you after class."

Madison and Ivy sank onto their lab stools.

And Madison still hadn't seen the note!

As Hart walked back into the classroom, Madison noticed that Ivy got distracted, so she took that opportunity to shove the note into the front pocket on her bag. She hadn't read it yet, but that wouldn't matter. She'd have plenty of time to look at it later in study hall or up in the media center or after school.

Chet gave her a thumbs-up from across the

classroom. Madison couldn't help but smile back at him. He was an advocate of anyone who got into trouble. And that was her right now . . . TROUBLE.

A while later, when class ended, Hart walked out with everyone else. Madison didn't have a chance to ask him about the note. Meanwhile Ivy had already stood up and approached Mr. Danehy's desk, ready to make her own plea bargain. Madison got up, grabbed her bag, too, and sat down in a chair at the front of the room.

"So, Miss Finn and Miss Daly. Which one of you would like to start with an explanation?"

Ivy raised her hand. "Ooh! Me."

Madison rolled her eyes.

"So this is how it happened, Mr. Danehy," Ivy explained, a smile on her face the entire time. "I was just sitting there listening to you tell us all about the science fair—which, by the way, I really want to par-ticipate in—when all of a sudden Madison Finn wrote this note and tried to pass it over to Hart Jones. It was totally not me. It was totally all her."

"And Mr. Jones, apparently. Shouldn't we get him in here, too, then?" Mr. Danehy asked the girls.

"No!" Ivy blurted. "Like I was saying, it was all Madison, and he had absolutely nothing to do with what happened."

"I see," Mr. Danehy said. He made a "hmmm" noise and then turned the floor over to Madison.

"Well," Madison tried to explain. "I was also

listening to you talk about the science fair when suddenly Ivy started to accuse me of having been passed a note or passing a note. Something like that. And I didn't have one. So I got flustered."

"What do you have to say to this, Miss Daly?"

"I can show you where the note is, Mr. Danehy. It's in her bag," Ivy said, grabbing at Madison's orange bag. "In that front pocket."

Madison pulled the bag back into her body. "I don't think so, Ivy," she said.

But Ivy wouldn't give up. Not only was she upset that Madison had scooped her troublemaking scheme, but she was way more upset because the boy she liked had passed a note to none other than Madison Francesca Finn.

Ivy lunged for Madison's bag a second time, only now she grabbed onto the side zipper. With one swift movement, she reached into the front pocket and pulled out the note.

Or, at least what she thought *was the note.*

"YOUNG LADIES! ENOUGH!" Mr. Danehy yelled. "Ivy, you can't just go probing into someone's personal property like that. Give that to me!"

He took the note from Ivy and looked it over.

"This looks like it took an awfully long time to write," Mr. Danehy said. "And what do you say to the fact that your name is on this note along with Madison Finn's name?"

"What?" Ivy said.

He held the note out for her to look at.

"I—I—don't know . . ." Ivy stammered. "What *is* this?"

MADISON FINN & IVY DALY
Friends Forever and Ever and Ever
For OUR eyes ONLY!!!

Madison hung her head. After all of her hesitating and procrastinating, *this* was the way Ivy finally got to see the letter.

By mistake.

"What *is* this, Maddie?" Ivy asked.

Mr. Danehy picked up his briefcase and started to exit his classroom. "The second bell will be ringing shortly, young ladies. I suggest you get to where you need to be."

Madison turned to Ivy. "I found it. During the snowstorm. In my attic."

"Do you remember writing this?" Ivy asked.

"Sort of," Madison admitted. "Do you?"

Ivy let out a deep sigh. "Whoa. This is weird. It's like having a flashback. How long have you had it?" Ivy asked.

"A while. Since last week."

"And you never showed it to me?" Ivy whined.

"It's not like we talk a lot," Madison replied.

"I can't believe you would open this without me,

when it says right here that we're supposed to open it together," Ivy said.

She grabbed the note, picked up her bag, and stormed out of the science room, leaving Madison all alone.

Chapter 14

The Letter

After Ivy discovered the letter in the pocket of my bag, she just took it and I raced after her and we ended up in the girls' bathroom down by Mrs. Wing's computer labs. I followed her into the bathroom because I had to talk to her. Even though she is the enemy, I felt bad. I don't wanna feel bad like that.

Ivy said that it didn't matter if we were friends or enemies, that a promise was a promise. And that I shouldn't have opened this letter alone.

I NEVER, EVER would have thought that Poison Ivy would care.

> After she left, I sneaked out and ducked
> into Mrs. Wing's lab. She never checks for
> hall passes, which is a good thing.

Madison closed the file on the letter. "This all started with his note," she said, digging into her bag's front pocket.

Madison pulled out Hart's note. She didn't have to actually read the note because she already memorized it. But it was nice to hold it and read it again.

> Finnster
> What is ur *e*-mail?
> Hart

This was a real note from Hart. She wanted to tell someone. . . .

Bigwheels!

Madison went into bigfishbowl.com and pressed NEW MESSAGE.

```
From: MadFinn
To: Bigwheels
Subject: Need Your Help, Pleez
Date: Mon 22 Jan 4:18 PM
```

Remember how I said in my last
e-mail that my week has been zanier
than zany? Guess what? It got even
CRAZIER. Okay, so Ivy has now seen

the letter. You were right about
showing it to her. It was weird b/c
she even seemed sad that I read it
before I showed it to her. Like
even though we're not friends
anymore, I'm supposed to keep old
promises. That's so hard.

But there is another note now that
is even more confusing! (Drumroll,
please.) It's from Hart. COULD YOU
JUST DIE OR WHAT?????

Okay, so I don't know if this note
means he likes me or what. It says,
"Finnster What is ur e-mail? Hart."

What do you think?

Yours till the math tests,

MadFinn

As Madison hit SEND, she heard the phone ring
downstairs. Mom yelled up, "Telephone!" and
Madison logged off and went downstairs to
answer it.

"Hey, Maddie!" Fiona gushed into the receiver.
"Chet told me you and Ivy got into some massive
trouble in science class today. Is it true?"

"Chet has a big mouth," Madison said.

"Well, yeah." Fiona giggled. "So tell me what happened."

Madison wanted to tell. But she had to leave out the whole part about Hart's note because neither Fiona nor Aimee knew about Madison's undying crush on Hart. And she had to leave out the part about the Ivy and Madison note from second grade because they didn't know about that, either. Maybe Madison would tell them later, but not now.

"Well, nothing really happened," Madison said. "I thought I saw her passing notes. But I was wrong."

"That's it?" Fiona said. "But Chet said you guys were so upset. And someone saw Ivy *crying* in the hallway."

"They did?" Madison asked.

"Well, I'm just glad that you didn't get into trouble and that everything is okay now," Fiona said.

"Where is Aimee tonight? I tried calling her," Madison asked.

"Ballet. Where else?" Fiona said.

Aimee had missed several classes because of the snowstorms, so she was eager to get back to practicing. She'd signed up for private lessons twice a week for a month. That meant Madison and Fiona would be seeing less of their other best friend, at least for a while.

Fiona hung up so she could surf the Web

and Madison went into the kitchen at home for a snack. Mom was emptying the dishwasher.

"Oh! Perfect!" Mom said. "I've got you! Let's run up to the attic for just a moment. I want to show you something I found."

Madison grumbled. She didn't feel like doing much of anything right now except eating peanut butter and crackers. She didn't feel like rummaging through Mom's work materials and organizing boxes. They'd been doing that for days!

But she still managed to follow Mom up the stairs.

Phinnie followed close behind, too.

"Take a look," Mom said, grinning as she pushed open the attic door. "What do you think?"

Madison's jaw dropped open. Mom had *completely* rearranged the attic. On one side there were still boxes and piles, but across the room, she'd covered an old sofa that was up there with a new blanket and added a reading lamp.

"So if we're feeling nostalgic or we just want to have a look around," Mom explained, "it won't be such a big production. So, quit standing there. Tell me, what do you think?"

Madison smiled. "Amazing."

"And I ordered some bookshelves so I can make a better filing system up here. And I was even thinking you might want to put your desk under this window at some point. Like a private room for studying. It's up to you."

Madison couldn't stop smiling.

"Oh! I almost forgot to tell you that Dad is on his way home. He should be back in Far Hills tonight. In fact"—Mom reached her arm out to check the time—"he should be pulling into our driveway in an hour or so."

Madison threw her arms around Mom and dashed back down the stairs. If Dad was coming, she wanted to dress up a little, or at least to get out of her school clothes. She put on some strawberry-kiwi lip gloss for the special occasion.

Dad took Madison out for Chinese food in downtown Far Hills, just the two of them. Stephanie had stayed behind in Denver to tend to more business. On the way home, Madison spilled the beans to Dad about everything that had happened with Hart's note. He sounded encouraging, although dads tend to be more cautious about such matters of the heart, and Madison knew that.

When Dad dropped her off after nine o'clock, Madison was exhausted. But she still found time to sneak back online for one last e-mail check.

```
From: Bigwheels
To: MadFinn
Subject: Re: Need Your Help, Pleez
Date: Mon 22 Jan 7:54 PM
```

You won't believe this, but it is
SNOWING like mad here right now!
We have a foot and a half in our
yard, and all the weather reports
now say that we're getting another
storm in Washington just like
yours! I don't ever remember seeing
so much snow! Now I know what
you were talking about last week.
What was that silly joke your
dad sent you? I wanted to tell
my mom. Resend it if you can.

So I read your note about Hart's
note. That is so weird he did
that. And I really think maybe
he is just trying to spend more
time with you because he likes
you, but I don't know for sure
if he means anything romantic.
I can't really tell. You haven't
told me what YOU think. Did he
say anything else? Sometimes I
wish I knew what he looks like.
He sounds so cute.

Write back sooner than soon?

Yours till the hockey pucks,

Bigwheels

p.s. I wanted to tell you something else about friends b/c you seem so sad about that old friend Ivy and I don't like hearing you be sad. What if we made up a secret name for us? You always say everyone else is a BFF, but what if I'm your BIFF? Best Internet friend forever? Hope you like it! C U L8R!

As she logged off, Madison felt warm all over, and not just because she had on her woolly monkey slippers. Even though she had to let go of a friend from the past, she had a BIFF to enjoy the future with—through snow, rain, and whatever bad weather came her way.

Mad Chat Words:

```
(@@)            You're kidding!
:>D             It's grrrrrreat!
:-~(            I'm going to cry
(::)(::)        Band-Aid (for boo-boos)
?4U             Question for you
911             Emergency
DLTM            Don't lie to me
HHOK            Ha ha only kidding
VF              Very funny
VVF             Very very funny
BTDT            Been there, done that
SWDYT           So what do you think?
W-E             What-ever
BIFF            Best Internet friend forever
```

Madison's Computer Tip

Sometimes it's easy to forget that whatever you write online can be seen by *anyone*. Even when I'm chatting in a private room, someone from bigfishbowl.com could be monitoring what is said. Or another member could be eavesdropping. **Don't write online messages that contain too much private information.** Sometimes when I send long e-mails to Bigwheels, I forget this rule. I write negative stuff about Ivy or her drones. I probably should be careful. What if Ivy were to read what I wrote?

Visit Madison at www.madisonfinn.com

From the Files of

Madison Finn

#7: Save the Date

Chapter 1

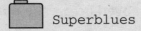

"Rain, rain, go away," Madison chanted. She typed in a brand-new file name.

 Superblues

Here it is the end of March and I have the seventh-grade superblues. Doesn't that sound like a song?

I can't seem to get ANYTHING done and I have this MEGA paper due for English honoring women's history that I haven't even started! I haven't done my Spanish homework for a week, and Señora Diaz is going to be so mad. I didn't know life was supposed to be stressed out in seventh grade. Is it just me or what?

Even Mom is superbusy these days with some new movie crew and assignment. Dad is

busy, too. Even when we have one of our
special dinners, he always has something
else on his mind besides me. His girlfriend,
Stephanie, says he's working on some new
Internet deal. Maybe he's nervous? Ever
since Mom and Dad's big D—divorce—last
year, things started getting busier and
weirder for all of us.

Rude Awakening: If I figure out how to
save time, how can I use it later? That
would really help with all this stuff I
have to do.

Madison closed her file and popped a brand-new
CD-ROM into her laptop. She easily booted up new
software called Calendar Girl that Dad had given her.

With the click of a few keys, Madison found her-
self at the main menu screen. A stardust trail chased
Madison's arrow cursor as it moved across the page.
Type flashed blue and pink.

Dear Diary Planner
Go to the Head of the Class
Homework Keeper
Extracurricular Time
Calendar Girl To Do
Friends Contact List

Madison stared at the screen. She didn't know
where to mouse-click first.

Drip.

She wiped a wet droplet off her hand. Was Phin drooling again?

Drip. Drip.

It wasn't drool at all.

Looking up over her head, Madison saw another pair of kamikaze drips before they landed. They were coming from the ceiling. The terrible rainstorm had made its way inside Madison's bedroom.

"MOM!" Madison screamed even louder than a thunderbolt. Phin jumped and dove off the bed for the closet. "MOM!" she screamed again.

Quickly Madison pulled her laptop to a dry area for safety. She moved her pillows and the afghan and grabbed her trash bucket to put on top of the bed. She hoped that would catch the drips. They were beginning to fall more steadily now, like a leaky faucet.

"Madison?" Mom was breathless from running up the stairs. "You know I hate it when you yell for me like that. What on earth—"

"We have a leak!" Madison screeched, pointing to the wet ceiling. Phin peeked out of the closet.

"Oh, no!" Mom wailed. "You've got to be kidding me!" She dashed out of the room.

"MOM! Where are you going?" Madison yelled. "Mom, get back here. My whole room is going to be underwater if you don't get back here!"

Mom returned a moment later with the phone and the yellow pages. She dialed up a contractor she'd called once before.

"Is this Dickson Fix-It?" Mom asked. "This is Francine Finn over on Blueberry Street. We seem to have this leak upstairs...."

Madison sat down near her desk and watched, helpless, as the drips kept dripping into her orange plastic wastepaper basket. Madison wanted to say, "Mom, why don't you call *Dad* instead?" but that wouldn't have been a proper suggestion. Not since the big D.

Dad *never* freaked out during emergencies like Mom did. During the winter, the boiler had stopped working and Mom almost exploded the house trying to fix it alone. Had Dad been around, it would have been repaired without a second thought. He would have had this roof leak solved in a flash.

Fwwwwackkkkkkkk!

A new bolt of thunder cracked. The rain started to fall harder again. So did the drips. Phin scooted into the closet again.

"What is going to happen to my room?" Madison cried. "My stuff is all going to be ruined. MOM! Aimee's coming over soon!"

Even though it was Sunday and a school night, Madison's best friend Aimee Gillespie was coming over to eat dinner and do homework. Aimee's parents had to go somewhere for a business dinner with some other booksellers. Her father's store, The Book Web, had won some kind of local business award.

Madison's other best friend, Fiona Waters, had been invited to come over for the study session too, but she had a family dinner to attend. So it was two neighborhood BFFs instead of three.

"Now, just calm down, Maddie," Mom said. "You can bring your laptop downstairs when Aimee comes. We'll move you into the den until this gets fixed."

Dingdong.

"Aimee's here NOW!" Madison squealed. "She's going to absolutely freak out when she sees this!"

Madison skipped downstairs to answer the front door as a very wet Aimee pushed her way inside.

"Oh my God! My mom had to *drive* me over here. It is soooo wet out!" Aimee cried.

Phinnie squirmed around on the wet floor by Aimee's feet, his tail squiggling. Even with all the rain, Phin could smell Aimee's dog, Blossom, all over her jeans. He sniffed and sniffed. Aimee just giggled and kept shaking her wet head. She looked like she was doing some kind of rain dance. As a ballerina, Aimee did *everything* with dancing flair.

"Here, use this, Aim," Madison said, handing Aimee a towel from the downstairs bathroom.

"Thanks!" Aimee said, still twirling. "So what's up?"

"My whole room is LEAKING!" Madison launched into a full explanation of the disaster in her bedroom.

"Whoa," Aimee said. "That sounds pretty bad."

5

She reached into her bag and pulled out a bottle of blue nail polish. The jar said, Are You Blue?

"What's that for?" Madison asked.

"I got it at the store today. I could paint your nails tonight," Aimee said with a wide grin. "This color will look so perfect on you."

"Really?" Madison asked.

"I think we should blow off homework and have a beauty night," Aimee said. "At least before we eat dinner."

"I have an English paper to write," Madison said.

"Yeah, but this will be more fun," Aimee argued.

"I guess you're right," Madison said with a giant smile. "I wanted to show you this new lip gloss I just bought, too. Let me get it."

Madison reached over for her orange bag, sitting on a table in the hall, and fished around inside. First she pulled out a few books, a green notebook, a pencil case, a pair of socks . . .

"What is all *that*?" Aimee said, laughing.

"Oh, just stuff I really need," Madison replied. She took out a calculator, a package of gum, a purple bandanna...

"Wait. I've never seen that scarf. When did you get that?" Aimee asked.

"Last month at the mall. I forgot I left it in here."

Madison still couldn't find the lip gloss, so she turned her bag upside-down and dumped everything else right onto the hall carpet. There on the carpet were two neon-colored rubber bands, two chewed-on pen caps, a pen that had just started leaking (luckily into an old tissue), a rabbit's foot key chain, and one large piece of light blue crumpled paper that appeared to be stuck to some chewing gum.

"Bummer!" Madison said. "I must have left it in my locker."

She was about to shove all of the objects right back into the bag when she noticed the crumpled paper. She unfolded the sheet quickly.

SAVE THE DATE.

Madison read the paper aloud. It was a permission slip for the class science field trip that she was supposed to have returned to her science teacher a week earlier.

"Oh my God, Maddie! You never handed that in?" Aimee said when she saw the sheet.

Madison bit her lip. "Is that a bad thing?"

"Well, it's after the deadline," Aimee said.

"Yeah, b-ut . . ." Madison stammered. "What do you mean, I can't go?"

"Usually they're pretty strict about deadlines," Aimee said.

"I am such a space case," Madison said, frowning.

"I'm sure you'll still be able to go. Just get your mom to sign the slip right now. She can explain to the teacher what happened," Aimee said.

"MOM!" Without missing a beat, Madison yelled

for her mother. "MOM!" She was determined to get her permission slip signed right now.

Mom flung open her office door with a huff. "Madison Francesca Finn, haven't I asked you a zillion times to please—"

"Mom, will you sign this?" She shoved the rumpled gum-stained blue slip and a ballpoint pen under Mom's nose.

"What is it?" Mom asked, grabbing the slip to read it. "'Save the Date'? Where did this come from?"

"Her book bag," Aimee chimed in.

Madison gave Aimee's left shoulder a thwack.

"I meant to give it to you before, Mom, but it got stuck—"

"I can see that," Mom said, fingers on the dried-up gum. She signed on the dotted line. "This trip is in a couple of days. Are you prepared? It says you have to do some research in advance."

"Oh no!" Aimee chimed in again. "That's just stuff we do during regular class. She's totally prepared for the trip. . . ."

"Next time you get one of these give it to me right away," Mom said.

Dingdong.

Mom threw her hands in the air. "Now, what?"